Dishonorably Discharged

A Love Story

By Desean Rambo

deseanrambo@boardgamemedia.com

Stay in the loop on future releases, updates, and special offers.

Join the exclusive email list today:

Click Here to Join

Also by Desean Rambo:

All's Fair in Love and Football Series

Dishonorably Discharged 2

Dishonorably Discharged 3

Wrestling the Russian

http://www.DeseanRambo.com

Available at eBook retailers near you!

1

SMACK.

That's the sound your skull makes when it bounces off a two hundred pound refrigerator. I was in a fight for my life. I had no idea how we got here.

"Get out of my face!" Justin blurted at me as he swung his arms wildly in my direction. I tried my best to take cover behind my arms but there is only so much a woman can do in a fight with a 6'4", 230 lb. Marine.

"Stop it!" I screamed. The pitch of my voice pierced through the apartment to no avail. I was getting beat to death by my newlywed husband.

Post-Traumatic Stress Disorder is a bitch to deal with. It's even worse when you are on the receiving ends of the blows. I had no idea what triggered Justin but I was feeling the full force of his rage. The usually stoic, mild-mannered, blue eyed, nice guy was now doing his best to try to take my life. I had to get out of here.

I fought. I fought and I fought some more. I scratched his eyes, grabbed his throat, and even kicked him in the groin. I tried anything to get some distance between me and my attempted murderer husband. I prayed a neighbor would hear me cry. I prayed he'd snap out of it. It felt like nothing was working.

Eventually a passerby heard the commotion seeping from our walls and called the police. In an instant, three years of marriage was down the drain.

The officers pleaded with me to press charges but I couldn't do it. There was something in my heart that still loved Justin. That something forgave him. He was not this way due to choice. The military is a complicated profession. Though I knew the stories, there was nothing I could do to make me fully understand what the reality of combat is like. That was, until that night.

Justin tried to get me back. He did. Several times. I wanted to stand strong but no matter what, it seemed fruitless. He had a way of being able to make you forgive him. My mother warned me several times, yet it happened anyway.

It started on Facebook. Every few days, he'd tend to my inbox like a plant he was watering. Each message was more and more contrite.

MESSAGE 1:

> *Hey Kaitlyn.*
>
> *I'm sorry. You know I didn't mean to do anything to you that would hurt you. I wish there was something I could do to make it right. If I could take it back, I would. I'm sorry, I need you.*
>
> *-Justin*

MESSAGE 2:

> *Hey Kaitlyn,*
>
> *I know you're not going to respond to this but please believe me. I am truly SORRY. You are the best thing that ever happened to me in my life. I cannot say sorry enough. If you never talk to me again in life I understand, but PLEASE find it in your heart to forgive me. I love you.*
>
> *-Justin*

MESSAGE 3:

> *Kaitlyn.*

Don't be mad at me. Again, I'M SORRY.

I think about you every single day. I really don't know what to do. Like I said, if there was anything I could do to go back in time and take it back, I would. I am truly sorry for my actions and I just want to let you know that no matter what happens, I will not stop loving you.

If you find it in your heart to forgive me as your husband then please give me one more chance. Just one more chance. I will never do anything to hurt you again.

-Justin

As much as my instincts told me to stay far away from the man who almost killed me, I just could not do it. At the end of the day, he was still my husband and we took vows, vows that included "for better or for worse, in sickness and in health." As far as I was concerned, Justin was sick and it was not his fault. Somewhere deep inside the gregarious, personable, humorous, fun guy I loved was still there. I had to see if I could rescue him. I felt that I owed him a second chance.

After approximately 90 days of silence, I finally responded:

Justin,

I want what happened between us never to happen again. You are still my husband. I know you did not mean your actions on that night. I will give you one last chance to prove to me you have changed. One chance and once chance only.

-Kate

We agreed to meet for dinner and drinks at a bar and grill. So many thoughts raced through my mind. I had no idea what he had been up to since the arrest. *Where was he working? Was he discharged? If we get back together, how are we going to make a living? Wait, where was he living? Did he move back in with his folks? Was he living in town? Was he in the barracks?*

My mind spun a thousand miles an hour as I drove to the spot. Cautious, I circled the restaurant to make sure he was inside before I got out. I wasn't taking any chances of being kidnapped in the parking lot. The more people there were around, the better.

There he sat alone, sipping on a glass of water with lemon, a man broken. It hurt to see him like this but it was the way things had to be. The five o'clock shadow along his jaw line matched the new bags underneath his eyes. Justin hadn't eaten or slept in weeks. It broke my heart to see my husband in this condition.

2

I wish I could say it was a cinematic stormy night with light rain and moonlight to set the mood, but it wasn't. There I sat in a semi-crowded bar across from my now almost-ex-husband, trying to decide how to start communicating with him again.

A waitress broke the silence.

"What will we be having?"

I glanced at Justin. He averted my eye contact as if to say he wasn't hungry. I ordered us two drinks. This was certainly not a dinner type of conversation. If anything, I wanted the option to throw my cash on the table and leave quickly if I had to.

Here's the thing. In life, there are rules and norms whether we believe that or not, whether they are ever spoken or not. In any relationship, there is one person that is the more dominant, more powerful person. There is the aggressor and the submissive, the leader and the follower. In this relationship, my husband had always been the leader. He was naturally strong, naturally outspoken and thoughtful. He could be trusted to lead us in the right direction when the time came for it. That was all before the incident. Ever since that night, the ball was in my court. I was suddenly the captain and he the lieutenant. This is a position I had never been before in any relationship but I was willing to try it. My marriage depended on it after all.

Justin didn't touch the alcohol I ordered. He sipped his water attentively as he studied my face. It was as if he wanted to say something but knew that a simple "I'm sorry" would never be good enough. I tried to understand. Whatever he was going through was more than I could imagine. He wasn't the same person anymore. It was as if there were two people living in his skin now. There was the kind, warm, loving man I knew and the cold, aggressive, bloodthirsty killer who saw things overseas that I could never imagine. No known trigger or switch changed the personalities. He was never sure which would speak on a moment-to-moment basis.

I broke conversation first. I could tell that's what he wanted me to do but as I said, I wasn't good at leading these types of things.

"So… what have you been up to?" I asked.

He grinned then spoke. "Just trying to live. Trying to make sense of this thing."

"What thing?" I replied.

"Life. I threw it all away," he said.

Justin always had a way of saying things plainly yet embedding a double meaning. I prodded him more.

"What do you mean by that?" I asked.

"It's all bad. My whole life has changed. I don't know which way is up," he continued. "I feel like I've died and I'm attending my own funeral over and over again."

Those were chilling words, especially since I knew he'd seen levels of death that most civilians only saw in movies. Marines had a special way of being desensitized to things like that.

"Why do you say that?" I asked as I sipped my Corona. I wanted him to know that above all else, I still cared. In a sad way, we both were victims to his Mr. Hyde.

"I lost it all. You know I got discharged right?" he asked.

It hit me like a ton of bricks. His career was over and it all happened in a matter of weeks. I knew there was a chance it could happen but I never really thought about it. Now, it was right in my face. He really lost everything.

I decided to drop the subject. The pain in his steel blue eyes was too much. I was starting to tear up as well. After all, we were still legally married. This affected us both.

“So where are you staying these days?” I asked calmly. I didn’t want to stick on the subject of money.

“With a buddy,” he answered.

“You can’t stay with your parents in Minnesota?”

“My mother already told me no,” he said. The pain was too much. He covered his face. A few seconds later, he started sniffling. “She said I was a piece of shit for what I did and I didn’t deserve to live. I’m not welcome in her home.” He paused between each word, struggling to get out audible sounds. The confession was too much. He had to excuse himself to get his emotions together. I wiped my face as he left.

How could I let him live like this? I asked myself. Everything was simply too much to deal with. *Yes, he hit you, but you’re alright. His life is ruined.* I didn’t see it then but the seeds were already beginning to sow for me to forgive him.

Justin returned a little more composed. He faked a smile.

“So is everything cool with you?” he asked. I could tell he didn’t want to go back down that lane so I dropped talking about his life. He was below rock bottom and we both understood that.

“Yeah. I’ve been working and taking my mind off things,” I said. He didn’t know it but I still stayed in the same apartment complex. I just moved to a different building on the backside of the property for security.

"That's good. That's good," he said. "You seeing anyone? Any new nice guys come to spice your life up?" He smirked. He always had a way of saying things like that. I knew what he really meant.

"No. We are still married. I'm not that type of girl."

"Just checking, just checking. Don't get defensive. I didn't mean you were that type of girl." He broke into a calmer tone. "About that, if you want to speak to a lawyer or whatever…" I cut him off. "Justin, I just need time to get my mind together. If I wanted a divorce, I'd get one. There are a lot of things I need to just think about, a lot of things that just need to take its time."

That answer pleased him. I just hoped and prayed he'd get the message. If things were going to work out, he'd have to put some serious overtime in. A couple of Facebook messages weren't going to do trick. A small silence came upon the table. I decided it was best if we called it a night at an amicable moment.

"Well it was good seeing you," I said as I stood up. He stood up too. I could tell he didn't know if he should try to hug me or not, but what the hell. We were still married. I gave him a quick embrace before I headed for the door. "Take care of yourself, Justin," I said to him. "I will," he replied.

***

The next few weeks were mundane. There were no dates, no late night conversations with Justin, just work. And work, and work, and work, and work. I threw everything I had into the office to keep my mind off my husband. I got one, two, then three months ahead on my reports. I reorganized my desk a dozen times. I started coming in early and leaving late. Anything that would fill time, I did.

I knew that if I had any sort of free time, the natural instinct would be to see Justin. *What was he doing? How was he living? Was he working yet? Did he trim that beard yet? How does he look with a full beard? How was he wearing his hair now?* Every secondary thought of every moment consisted of him yet I repressed it with work.

My girlfriends knew the drill. They tried their best to get me off him. Tricia, my bestie since high school, was now living about an hour away and working as a buyer for a clothing store. I always knew if I needed her, I could call but there was never enough time since I had let work overtake my life.

"Girl, all that working isn't healthy," Tricia blared to me over the speakers of my cell phone. She was doing her job as a best friend and trying to look out. The funny thing is, a big girl like Patricia was telling me what was and wasn't healthy. "I'm healthy. I'm more than healthy," she boasted. For a big girl, she had the confidence to match. Sometimes I close my eyes and imagine I'm talking to the actress Mo'Nique.

"You know what girl? Put all that work to the side and come out with us tonight. Me and some of my people are going out. Come hang out with us." She was right. I needed to decompress. It was nine weeks of evading Justin on Facebook and another four of working nonstop. I was running on emotional fumes.

"Ok. I'm coming down. Just text me the address." Two hours later, I was in the car and meeting Tricia and some of her work buddies at a waterfront lounge. Patricia knew how to be the center of attention while keeping everyone in a good mood. She was always the master of ceremonies. Tricia's friend from work, her friend's date, and I rounded out the group. After about an hour or so of live music, we decided to hit a restaurant a few blocks down.

Tricia's friend and her date walked in front while we lagged behind. Tricia pulled me close to her. She didn't want them to hear what she was about to tell me.

"Girl… he's a good man. He owns a limo and he's got no kids."

That's when it hit me. Trici's friends weren't dating. The girls were playing matchmaker. This was a sneak attack!

I really wasn't up for meeting anyone. Besides, he was not my type. I have nothing against the brothers. I just preferred what I preferred and I was at the age where I no longer wanted to deviate from the look I personally liked. Tricia should have known me better than this by now.

We ended up at a quiet little steak house on a corner block. The girls worked in unison to set it up so we sat at a secluded round table with me directly next to their male friend.

"So Rashon, I hear that you're single," Tricia started. "And you own your own limo, right?"

He sat up straight as if he was being called on in a game show. He wasn't ugly but he wasn't my type and clearly too nervous to get his own dates. "Yeah," he replied. Tricia and her friend smiled at me. I wasn't amused but I didn't want to crush their friend's expectations.

"So you're single, right?" Tricia's friend asked him. "Yeah." He smiled at me. His desperation was cute in a 5th grade way. As an adult, I was offended they would set me up with such a socially awkward person. On what planet did I ask for this? When did I tell Patricia I was looking for a date?

Whatever. I went along with it anyway. Patricia would get the brunt of my frustration privately. A few minutes in, they had a genius idea. "You two can talk privately. We'll wait at the bar," Tricia said. *Great,* I thought, *Now, I have to share a meal with this guy. Let's get it over with.*

It wasn't that bad. He was a nice guy. He was too nice. He had no edge, no spark, no humor like Justin. Rashon was a shy, sheltered guy who would make some woman really happy one day. That woman was not going to be me.

We sat for about twenty minutes, talking mostly about family and work. Rashon had actually gone to high school with my first cousin, and used to work in the same building as my mother at a different company. They both would later confirm they had seen Rashon around but only directly interacted with him once or twice, which only proved my theory on him. *He was a nice guy, but in a family way.*

"We should get Tricia," I said as our conversation dwindled. Tricia wasn't going to come save her girl. She thought I was enjoying this sneak attack because I hadn't cut or screamed on the poor guy.

Rashon agreed and let me excuse myself to get the rest of our party. We rejoined him at the round table to exchange goodbyes. "Wait! You two should exchange numbers!" Tricia yelled. *Great.*

"You don't even know my situation. What if I was married, or had kids?" I asked.

"You have to be good people if you know them," he quickly answered.

Great. I couldn't let the little guy down easy. I unwillingly gave him my number and walked quickly to my car without saying goodbye to Tricia or her friend.

She texted me as I drove home. I let her have it.

> *"He's practically part of my family. He went to school with my cousin and worked with my mother."*

"Why didn't you tell me you were going to sneak attack me?"

"Just because I was polite doesn't mean I liked him."

"I just went along with I because he was in my face and I didn't want to disrespect you or your friends."

"There will be no second date. I'm not going to call him."

"It's okay. I owe you one."

Tricia is a great friend and all, but she didn't know what I was really going through. I didn't have a man in my life at the time because there was already a man in that spot, a man whose spot never got taken. My husband.

3

The whole issue gave me the inspiration I needed to move forward in my love life. If I wasn't going to make decisions and follow my heart, people around me proved they were ready to make those decisions for me. Rashon is a nice guy and all, but I could never see myself with someone like that. He didn't do it for me. I liked a type and I already had it. It was time to reconnect with my husband.

I had no idea what Justin had been up to in the four months since the incident and my thoughts ran wild. *Was he still couch surfing? What buddy was he staying with? Was it a female? Was he moving on? Where was he working? What was he doing with that beard?!*

At work, things just got miserable. As much as I tried to stay ahead, work kept coming to replace what I already cleared off the table. Being a professional tax preparer, you expect businesses to wait until the last minute to file taxes but this was too much. I was finding more and more work as fast as I could look for it. This was not healthy.

Rashon texted me a few times. I guess he didn't get the hint. I made the mistake of replying to his first text, which gave him a false green light into my inbox. How many unanswered "Good Morning" tweets can a guy send before he gives up?

One afternoon after work, I had enough and decided to text Tricia to end it.

> *"Tell your boy Rashon to move on. I'm not interested."*
>
> *"Yes, I responded to one text. That doesn't mean I was interested."*
>
> *"I didn't respond to any others."*

"He's a nice guy but he isn't for me. Introduce him to someone else."

Tricia campaigned for Rashon but eventually she got it. This is why you don't let your friends run your love life.

I had some campaigning to do of my own. I had to figure out what Justin was up to and decide a plan of attack to get him back without looking crazy to my friends and family. Everyone had their own opinion but forget them. This was my life and I was going to do what I wanted.

There was one easy way to catch up on his life. You guessed it. Facebook. With a bottle of wine, a night with nothing to do, and the new Elle Varner CD, I felt like nothing could stop me. I was about to crack this case like *Murder, She Wrote.*

That night I logged in with my mind on a mission: figure out what the heck Justin's been up to and if there are any new chicks I'd have to regulate. I surfed around his page intently, checking every wall post four months deep just in case. Anything that was a little too personal, more than a friendly "Hi!" deserved a deeper search. I checked page after page, males and females, to get the scoop on Justin's new life.

It took roughly four hours of spider webbing through photo albums, posts, and wall posts to determine there was nothing to worry about. Justin was clean. Apparently he got a job at a local restaurant as a short order cook and was staying with one of his Marine buddies. There were new females, no new relationships, just a bunch of pictures of him and his former Military buddies. I could calm down.

Up next was a plan of action. *Should I just pop up at his job? Should I send him a message? Should I call him? How do I not look desperate?* All of those questions needed answers. I deeply thought about the repercussions of each choice. In the end, popping up at his job made the most sense. I quickly Googled the address and called it a night.

***

The next morning, I was on pins and needles. This had to work. Not only did it have to work, it had to work correctly. I had to make sure I ran into him, but make it look like an accident. I put on one of my favorite body hugging outfits, a tight black blouse with a thigh-hugging pencil skirt, and waited the day out at work.

Work went by much faster than I expected. I don't even remember what we did. I just remember walking in and walking out a nervous wreck. I trotted to my car repeating the same sentence aloud: *"Don't mess this up, Kate. Don't mess this up."*

I nervously inserted the key in my little Honda and left the parking lot, brimming with anxiety. He didn't know I was showing up. His reaction is not going to be planned. While everything looked all right on Facebook, four months is a long time. I knew he still had love for me but I was about to find out if he still loved me… or so I thought.

It took me ten minutes to arrive at the Burger Shack Justin was working at. After another ten minutes of talking myself into it, I finally got the courage to walk through the door. It was now or never. Sweat dripped down the small of my back. I was super nervous. I killed time with the hostesses at the front so I could get a peek into the kitchen. I couldn't see him.

I sat down, ordered, and played on my phone just in case he were to show up. I did not want to be caught looking for him. Twenty minutes later, my stomach was full, I was bored, and there was still no sight of my husband. I peeked in the kitchen every chance I could get. He wasn't back there. The trip was a bust.

I would repeat the same routine four times and not see Justin. It was beginning to irk me. Maybe his schedule was different from mine. Maybe I had the wrong location. Maybe I had bad luck. *Maybe it just wasn't meant to be*, I thought.

That was until the fateful evening that changed everything.

That evening I was driving back from the Burger Shack, once again frustrated I couldn't find Justin. It was an average night. Not too many cars were on the road. It wasn't raining or cold. It was a normal fall day.

BOOM! BOOM!

I must have run the car over something on the right side. I felt the car shake violently. This was just what I needed, a flat tire. I pulled over to assess the damage. The car was fine thankfully, but now there was the issue of the flat tire on the rear passenger side. It wasn't fully flat but I needed to do something before it was. I didn't feel like trying to change the tire by myself, so I decided I could drive it long enough to get to a gas station and buy some Fix-A-Flat. If I knew what I know now, I would have probably changed the tire. That singular decision changed everything in my life.

I pulled over at a BP station. I'd never been to this specific location before. I forgot how I was dressed as I briskly walked through the automatic doors, cleavage bursting out of my white blouse from the black bra underneath.

Then I saw him.

The station attendant was a 6'3" tall glass of milk made right from the mold I like. He looked like a blue-collar version of Bradley Cooper with his chiseled jaw lined by dark brown stubble, his hair going every which way, and tight biceps peaking out of a white t shirt. In a weird way, he looked like Justin, if Justin *really* stopped grooming and had brown eyes. I knew it right then that this stop was going to be bad for my marriage.

"Excuse me!" I yelled over to him.

I caught him off guard, his back partly turned to me. I could tell my outfit startled him when he got a good look. I supposed he liked what he saw.

"Can I help you?" he said as he leaned over the counter. Those biceps were going a good job of keeping him upright and I was enjoying the view.

"Fix-A-Flat. Do you have it?" I asked.

He immediately left the counter to join me on the other side. "Flat tire?" His voice was strong and filled with bass, unlike anything I heard from Justin lately.

"Yeah," I replied. It was time to play up the damsel in distress. Maybe Bradley Cooper would fix my flat and maybe some other things, free of charge.

"Is that your car?" he said as he pointed towards my lonely Honda Civic. The streetlights illuminated it like a little white bean.

"Yeah. I hit something on the road." I said.

"It just happened? Fix-A-Flat isn't going to do anything if you've got a hole. Let me take a look at it and we'll see what can be done." We walked out to the car. The tire was completely flat now.

Bradley grabbed his steel stubbly jaw with a perplexed look. I'm not sure if he was thinking about the car or checking me out in the reflection. Either way, I adjusted myself just in case. He broke the silence. "Do you have a donut?"

"Yeah," I replied. I beeped the car and hopped inside to pop the trunk. He looked through my trunk while I adjusted myself in my visor mirror. A moment later, he came to my car door. A little smirk was on his face. "You don't have a jack? What's the point of the spare if you can't use it, young lady?"

"I know. I lost it somewhere," I replied.

"I have one inside. Let's get it. You don't need to sit in the car alone at this hour."

We slowly walked back to the station. A manly confidence lulled in the air. He turned to me again with that sly little smirk. "Do you even know how to change a tire?" I could tell by the way he asked, he was setting me up.

"No," I admitted.

"You gon' learn today!" Bradley did his best impression.

OH. MY. GOD. This white boy did not just break out a Kevin Hart joke on me. I think I felt my body temperature rise thirty degrees as he laughed at me with those bold brown eyes. I had to know his real name.

"James," he said confidently. He must get hit on all the time. "And who are you? You got a name, young lady?" he asked.

"Kaitlyn. You can call me Kate though. Hey, this is a bit odd but has anyone told you that you kind of look like…"

"Bradley Cooper." He cut me off. "I get that all the time." He drew out the word "all" to emphasize his point.

He disappeared into the back of the store before reappearing with the jack. "Got it. Class is in session, girly," he teased. This guy was a jerk, but wow was he a hot jerk.

We went back to the car and I watched as James lifted it up on the jack and spun a couple of the lug nuts off. His back muscles rippled with every move and I stared with each moment. He turned back to me.

"Come down here. You need to learn how to do this." I grabbed the long tire iron and slid it on the fitting nut. I twisted the iron until the nut fell to the ground. James was silent the entire time. Perhaps he took the opportunity to enjoy the view of my cleavage bouncing about.

I handed him the tire iron back and he changed the tire in a matter of minutes. He pointed out things here and there as he went along, but I was too distracted to listen. I just nodded as he did his thing.

"You can take the bad tired to a tire shop. They might be able to plug it for you," he said.

"Thank you so much," I replied.

"No problem." He smirked once again and started to head back to the store. I had to stop him.

"Hey, James?"

He turned back to me. That slick grin was still on his face. He already knew what the deal was.

"Do you want to call me sometime?" I asked. This was a bit forward but I figured no one would know if I was rejected. It was just him and me.

"Sure," he replied. I quickly gave him my number and thanked him once more before heading home. I knew that I still needed to find Justin but in the meantime, a girl has to look out for herself. Besides, if my car ever broke down again I knew exactly whom I was going to call.

4

I waited four days. James never called. If only he had Rashon's false confidence. A guy like James must have women galore to choose from. What did he need me for?

That's how I would have thought if I wasn't in my situation. My estranged husband was impossible to find outside of Facebook, and my bestie was trying to set me up with a guy with the personality of a banana peel. I wasn't totally lonely but it was time to jump out of the frying pan and into the fryer, if you know what I mean.

I sent James the first text on the fourth day. I never contact first but this was a special exception.

"Hey what's up? ☺"

Four minutes later, he responded.

"Hey!"

"What are you doing?"

It totally felt like high school again. Goodness, I hadn't played the phone tag game in years.

"Chillin."

I really wasn't up for the one word text game. I'm sure he was sending these texts with that stupid aloof smile of his.

"Do you know who this is?"

I was trying to get conversation going. I was sure he would send a one-word answer. Two minutes later, my phone beeped.

"Yes."

Darn it. I wasn't up for this game all night but if he wanted to engage, I figured I'd see how far this would go.

"Can you write more than 1 word responses?"

Two minutes later, he replied. *"Yes."*

It was time to turn the tables.

"I know you aren't the brightest bulb in the box but come on!"

"*LOL*" was all he sent back. I'm sure he wasn't laughing anything beyond that stupid smirk. My phone beeped again.

"Says the girl who can't change a tire..."

Finally! I got something out of him. I'm not sure how these things usually go. I don't remember the last time I was texting someone I liked. I do remember not having to be the one courting though.

"So what's up? What are you fixing today?"

"Nothing today. That's two words."

"Technically five but no one is counting."

"LOL. What are you doing?"

"Waiting for you to call me."

"Do you want me to call you?"

"Yes."

"What if I only say one word?"

"I will hang up LOL."

"No you won't."

"Try me."

"Ok."

"Call me in five minutes."

"Ok."

It was done. Texting was fun and all, but you don't really know a person unless you can hear their tones and voice inflection. Besides, texting was taking too long. I was trying to do something fun to take my mind off work and Justin. Texting was not what I had in mind.

Five minutes passed and no call. Maybe I was too desperate. Maybe he forgot. Maybe he just didn't like me like that.

Screw it, I thought. I'd pass time on Justin's Facebook page. I still hadn't been able to run into him since learning where he was working. Maybe I could get some new information. If I had his number I'd just call him, but he never had a cell phone. He always said they were a waste of time and routed all his calls to his friends or me and worked us like mini secretaries. That's the thing about him. He was always walking his own path whether that be not having a phone... or dating a black girl.

Back to Facebook. I logged in and quickly clicked to his page.

Yes, this was now my life. On a regular Tuesday night when I should be enjoying the company of my lover, I was now making love to the illuminated dim from my MacBook. This was now an everyday occurrence to keep my mind off things.

Bam! Got it. I found a photo of Justin at work with the caption "chilling on the noon shift." He was making one of his patented childishly cute faces in the photo. I noted the time and decided I would pop up on him in a few days wearing my best freak 'em dress. Then it happened.

Ding!

What was that?

Ding!

A little window popped up on the lower right hand side of the page. It was Justin, talking to me in Facebook chat. I totally forgot that you could talk to people in real time on Facebook. I almost never used it. However there he was, flashing in the little window on my screen.

> *"Hey! What's up?"*

I didn't know what to do. Should I play it cool? Should I ignore him? Nah, I couldn't ignore him because obviously he could see that I was online. Since he had no phone, I knew this was probably as close to a conversation as I could have with him for a while. I decided to keep my cool and be cordial.

"Hey! How have you been?" I sent back. I could feel the excitement in my facial expression.

> *"Chilling. What are you doing on here?"*

He pulled my card that fast. He obviously knew what was up. I played dumb regardless. The last thing I needed was for him to know I was e-stalking him.

> *"Looking at some photos of my sister and the babies! What's new with you. Long time no hear."*

> *"Awesome. Killing time before sleep. Yeah long time ☹"*

There was that darn sad face. I sent back, *"So how have you been? What are you doing?"*

> *"Working at Burger Shack. I'm sure you heard."*

"Glad to hear that you're working."

"Yeah. But I"

He stopped. I pressured him on.

"You what?"

"I don't know how to say this," he started. *"I reallllly miss you."*

"I miss you too." I sent back, tears starting to well up in my eyes. Why were we reduced to this? It was time to cut straight to the point. I continued.

"We need to go out. Let's do something," I sent. It was worth a shot.

"Yes. That would be good," he sent back.

We chatted for about an hour on there about life, our relationship, and random topics like Kanye West and Kim Kardashian. I always appreciated his perspective on things. His realism kept me balanced. I think it's what made uswork. We decided that we'd go mini golfing that weekend and that I'd meet him at his friend's place before we left. I still didn't know what to expect or how far down this road I was prepared to go, but it was time. Almost five months had passed and there was no other serious contender in sight. I didn't care what my family or friends said. I was going to try to make it work again with my husband.

***

"Girl, you're crazy!" Tricia blared back at me on the phone.

I was swerving down the highway en route to Justin's friend's house. I decided I wasn't going to tell her about the date until I was already half way there so that I couldn't be talked out of it. She still didn't know about James. Not that she should.

"Tell me again what you're doing?" Tricia asked, like a teacher scolding an unruly child.

"I'm doing on a date with my *husband.* Calm down," I snapped back.

"I know he's your husband but don't forget he almost killed you, girl. You have to be smarter about this. Does anyone even know where you're going?"

She was right. Maybe I should have told someone but they all would have talked me out of it. It had been five months. I was lonely and possibly thinking out of desperation instead of using my brain.

"Fine, I'll text you the address," I said to oblige her.

I hung up minutes later and texted her Justin's new address. His buddy lived in a quiet little neighborhood in the suburbs. All of the homes were one or two stories with perfect earth tone vinyl siding and at least two cars in the driveway. It was a regular upper middle class spot.

I cruised my little Civic down a side road and onto the street with the name Justin gave me. His buddy's home was a one story white house, lined with a basketball hoop and several little shrubs. Justin's black Mustang was parked outside, perfectly washed and detailed. I always wondered which one of his black girls he loved more, me or that darn car.

I dressed sexy for the occasion: Vans shoes, regular twill pants, and a body-hugging sweater to accentuate my figure. Though this was my husband, and he's seen the goods before, it's always good to remind him. Five months is a long time.

I hopped out and knocked on the door. The butterflies mounted. I couldn't wait to see him. *Wait, how should I greet him? Should I hug him? Kiss him?*

There was no time for questions. The door immediately swung open and there was the man I loved.

He was much better looking than the last time I saw him. He grew out of the high and tight haircut, sporting more of a sophisticated civilian look, with a light beard, which was neatly trimmed. He smelled good too. His cologne was oaky but sweet at the same time. He was dressed in a white button up, khakis, and boat shoes. He was looking amazing. I flung into his arms and gave him a big warm embrace, the first one in a long time. It felt good. It felt right.

We got in the Mustang and headed to the mini golf spot. It was a quiet spot that high school kids would frequent. The clubhouse building had all the arcade games one would expect with cheesy cartoons painted on the walls. Oh well. It didn't matter what we were doing as long as we were spending time together.

We grabbed our clubs and headed out to the course. It was the first time we had done anything together in at least six months. The moment had me thrilled and anxious at the same time. "You ready to lose?" Justin smartly quipped at me.

"If I lose, I'm going to do you like Tiger Woods wife," I said as I jokingly swung the club at him. The joke hit a little too close to reality for him. He looked nervous I might actually club him in the head.

Ding! Ding!

My phone went off. It was Tricia with another text message.

"Are you okay?"

I quickly texted her back and put my phone on silent.

"You good?" Justin asked as I sent the text.

"I'm fine. That was just Tricia," I said. "She was worried about… this." The look on his face was one of disappointment. I could tell he felt he was on trial all over again. He was quiet for a moment before speaking.

"Give me your phone. I want to talk to her," he said.

"Nah. You're good," I said. "I told her everything is fine."

"I just want her to know I'm not some sort of monster," he said. "I understand everyone's concerns but they need to hear from me too. They don't know that wasn't me."

"I understand," I said. There was nothing more I could add. I wanted to change the topic as quick as possible. "Let's talk about something else."

We went around the course trading shots while I kept the conversation light. This was not the time to think about other people. This was supposed to be about us. After all, we were still legally married. Justin hit a shot that just missed a hole in one. I took the opportunity to playfully squeeze him on the bicep. The best way to get over the past was to get back under one another.

He lit up after that as we continued our night. I would make a good shot and he'd give me a congratulatory hug, lingering just a second too long. It was clear both of our minds were on how to get back to our physical relationship too.

Buzz! Buzz!

My phone went off as I aimed up a shot.

"You need to go?" Justin asked.

"I'm fine. Tricia can calm herself down," I answered.

After completing the course, we sat down in the cheesy game room to spend more time together. It was good just to reconnect. I gazed into his big blue eyes, totally silent for a few moments. It felt like I was getting to know the man I loved all over again. We held hands as our conversation picked up off the course.

"So what do you think?" Justin asked.

"What do I think about what?" I answered.

"Us," he said.

"I like this," I said. "I don't want to mess this up. Whatever this is."

"What are we doing?" he said back. "It's obvious we still love each other. I will do whatever it takes, Babe. Just give me a chance to show you I've changed. I've been doing my therapy, staying in my routine. I haven't had any flashbacks or anything. I just want my life back. I just want my wife back."

I hushed him. I wanted to be sure not to let him in that quickly. I wanted to enjoy the moment without making things even more complicated than they had to be. I just wanted him to understand that this was going to be a slow burn. Nothing good comes easy.

Buzz! Buzz! My cell phone went off again. I ignored it. Justin shrugged. He knew it was Tricia.

"Maybe I should get you home," he said. "I don't want your friend calling the police on me."

"Stop it!" I told him. "She's just overprotective, that's all."

"I really wish you'd let me talk to her," he answered.

"I really wish you'd get a phone," I said. "You know what. That's a good idea. Maybe one day we all can go out and put everything out in the open. That way, everyone can say what they need to say. We can get everything off our chests then."

I squeezed his large, warm hands as hard as I could.

"Ok," Justin said. "That might work." He was never one to go completely along with anything. He started to dart my eye contact. Something was on his mind.

"Are you alright?" I asked.

"Your mother…" he began, "…what am I supposed to say?"

"Nothing. I told her everything she needed to know," I assured him. The truth was, I did tell my mother everything, but I also *kind of hinted* that I wasn't going to see Justin again.

The game room started to close down. We decided to call it an early night. It was still before midnight, but these times were different. As we sped down the highway in the Mustang all I could do was reminisce on the old times, those times when we would go on dates and come back home to vigorous love making marathons. Despite how much I ached and how much I wanted to pounce on his Greek sculpture of a body, I knew that tonight wasn't the night. The little girl between my legs would have to chill for now.

We didn't say much on the ride back, just the kind of odd small talk you have with a distant relative, not your former lover.

We got back to his buddy's place so I could pick up my car. It felt odd. Normally we'd rush in the house to handle our business but this time, we slowly walked to my car and shared a long, warm hug. He kissed me on the forehead. I looked him deep in his eyes, then said that hard goodbye and got in my vehicle. It was one of the hardest things I had to do but it was right to drive away.

Everything felt better. Things finally felt like they were making sense a little now. I felt real remorse from Justin. The possibility of a new beginning was there.

Until it happened.

5

I finally got a chance to check my phone as I headed home on the highway. I was shocked by what I read.

It was James, not Tricia, blowing me up all night. He finally got the nerve to call back. I was already high off all of the attention from Justin earlier, so I decided to see what the magic mechanic James had to say.

> **CLICK* "Hello this is… never mind you know who it is. Call me back!" *CLICK**

That was about all I expected to get out of him, Mr. Good-Looking-With-No-Brain. Still, he intrigued me. There was something about him that was untamed and rough around the edges. I yearned to explore. I took a minute to compose myself and stop blushing before I called back.

"Hello?" he said. It sounded like he may be asleep or confused. He probably forgot he left the message in the first place.

"Hey, this is Kate."

"Katie! Kate. Yeah!" He perked right up. He seemed overly excited for some reason.

"So you called?" I said.

"Yeah. Sorry about the delay," he replied.

"I thought you forgot about little old me," I said. "What were you doing? Talking to your other chicks?" I teased.

"Yeah. I had a fight with the baby momma," he joked.

"You have kids?" I replied.

"Nah. Nah," he said.

"But you said baby momma…" I responded.

"Yeah. I'm a doggie daddy. My ex took my dog. Long story," he explained. It was actually kind of refreshing to hear that a big burly dude like that would show that kind of affection for a puppy.

"Ok. I see. How cute. What are you doing now?" I asked.

"Waiting for you," he said. There was a twinge of intrigue in his voice. Was Bradley Cooper inviting me over for a nightcap? He continued. "What are you doing right now?"

"I'm driving home from a friend's house."

"Perfect. I'll text you the address." He immediately hung up. He knew what he wanted and didn't beat around the bush. I could feel my body temperature boil. I decided why not get it popping? No one would know and technically, Justin and I were still separated. Besides, the dangerous stranger always has an extra aura of sexiness around him.

A minute later, the text came in with the address. It was really close to the direction I was already heading. This was too perfect.

I pulled over and ran into a Walgreens on the way over. I had to run into the ladies' room to get myself together. I adjusted my makeup and hair to make sure it was on point before I continued. I made sure the girls were plunging out underneath the sweater. I wanted to look not just hot but *hawt*. I needed him to want to devour me as soon as he laid eyes on me.

I bought a pack of gum and some lip gloss, then ran back to the car. What was I doing? I was crazy. My physical needs were controlling me but at this point, I no longer cared. This wasn't going to be a serious thing. This was a onetime thing that both of us clearly wanted.

The address was about six blocks from the Walgreens. I drove over to the small community lined with townhomes everywhere. It had limited parking and only a few streetlights. James stayed in a skinny little townhome sandwiched between two other identical ones. It was almost midnight and I was dolled up and ready to go. I called him to let him know I was outside before parking in a neighbor's spot and tiptoeing to his door.

He flicked on his light and peeked out the adjacent window. I could see the light line his jaw so slightly, the brown beard sticking out. He smiled then opened the door. He had on a plain white Hanes T-shirt and dark pants.

"What's up, Miss Jones?" he said. His spot was nice for being so small. There were black granite countertops, brand new appliances, and matching dark furniture complete with red and gold accent pieces around. He had great taste, or a girlfriend.

"Why are you calling Miss Jones?" I asked.

"Cleopatra Jones. You remind me of her. Have you ever seen that movie?"

"No," I said. I was familiar with it, but I'm not sure why he knew that. I wasn't expecting that reference from a guy like him. "Nice place," I continued.

"Do you want the tour?" he said. I knew that would end in his bedroom, which my nerves weren't ready for yet. I knew what I wanted, because the perspiration was starting to build.

"In a minute. How do you know Cleopatra Jones?" I asked.

“Foxy Brown,” he responded. “I was a big fan of hers. I watched all those movies back in the day.” He turned to the fridge and retrieved a bottle of champagne. “You want a drink?”

“I’m good,” I said. “One. I’ll take one,” I corrected myself. Alcohol wouldn’t hurt anything at this point. “So you like black girls?” I inquired as he poured our drinks.

“I love *women,*” he responded. It was the typical answer. He wasn’t about to get in the cookie jar without admitting he wanted some chocolate.

I pressed him playfully. “But do you typically go for black girls?”

“I’ve been with black girls before,” he said. “I never had a problem with any woman as long as she’s cool. Black girls are fine by me,” he joked. “Truth be told, you don’t even know who Cleopatra Jones is. I’m not even sure you’re black right now.” James had a bit of soul to him. It was obvious he had to have grown up around a lot of black people.

“What’s your background?” he asked as he slid me my glass. We stood in his tiny kitchen now, face to face as we sipped.

“I’m black,” I replied.

“I know that, but where are your people from?” he asked again.

“I don’t really know. I think some are from Haiti or Jamaica, and the rest were brought over here from Africa.”

He nodded. “I can see the Jamaican.”

“How so?” I asked.

“It’s all in your hips and your ass.” He smirked. “Can you dutty wine?”

"No!" I laughed. "Hold on. This is too good. I have to show you." He grabbed his phone out of the wall charger. His lock screen was his puppy, a miniature pinscher with black fur and light brown patches.

"Aww. You must really love your dog," I commented.

"You don't even know," he said. "My ex is keeping me from him. We bought him together but when it ended, she decided she was going to get at me by using him. One day she just told me straight up, buy another puppy. Eff that. That's my man. I'm going to get him back." The passion in his voice was amazing.

"Awww," I said.

"Crazy ass white girl, in case you're wondering," he added. "The sex was bomb, but she was a headcase. I should have seen it coming. Anyways, on to what we were doing. You are about to learn how to dutty wine!"

He browsed YouTube on his phone for a minute before loading up a Sean Paul song, *Temperature.* It played through the phone speakers, filling the silence in the little kitchen.

I got the right temperature to turn you onnnnnnn ooooooh

James moved in close. His brown eyes were inches from my face, the Superman jaw just as close. He grabbed me by the hips, his rough and callused hands pressing into the flesh exposed by the bottom of my sweater.

"You have to move your hips like this," he said as he twisted me from side to side. "You have to go with the beat."

I breathed in deeply as he pressed against me, firmer and firmer. I moved my hips to the beat. He was so slick. He knew exactly what he was doing. He glanced down as my chest bounced with each pound of the beat. He looked deep into my eyes and smirked.

"Am I doing it ri-" He put his finger on my lips to cut me off.

"Shhh..." He pulled me close to his massive, warm body and kissed me deeply. I closed my eyes and melted. The tall, beautiful stranger gripped me tighter and tighter as we kissed deeper and deeper.

I felt his warm hands make their way underneath my sweater. He grazed his hands up my side, exploring more and more flesh. His right hand slid over my bra and grazed the bulging breast tissue. Things were getting hot and heavy. My body temperature was rising. Other things were rising as well. I stopped him.

"How about you give me the official tour?" I said. We both knew where it was heading.

He pulled back and smiled. "Sure."

He quickly led me around the little townhouse as he pointed out little mementos. He was a big fan of lacrosse, not that it mattered. It was interesting to see his framed photos and ticket stubs from events he went to in the past. It was also more comforting to know he wasn't just some strange man who fixed things and picked up girls.

He led me up a narrow staircase to his master bedroom. Once again, it was very fashionable for a man. The red sheets matched all of the accents in the home along with the pillows. James sat on the edge of the bed and pulled his phone back out.

"Is this what you do for every girl?" I asked.

"What?"

"Get them in your room and then play YouTube videos?" I teased.

"Oh. Nah. Nah. I was trying to pull something up on my phone," he said.

Yes. With a hot and bothered female standing two feet in front of him, in his own bedroom with nipples poking out of her sweater, this guy was seriously checking his phone. I never gave him credit for being the smartest man that I met, but I was here for a reason and that wouldn't be denied. I sat down on the bed next to him.

"Why'd you invite me over?" I hinted.

"Because I wanted to see you," he said. "Texting and everything is fine, but I like being around a person. You know, being able to see them, smell them, *touch them...*"

"I totally agree," I said. His eyes were still locked on that darn phone. I couldn't see the screen. Whatever he was doing, he was totally enthralled.

"What are you doing?" I asked.

"Just wait *one minute...*"James replied.

"Come on..." I said as I grabbed his arm. I squeezed his strong biceps and began rubbing on his shoulder.

"*One second...*" he continued. I started to smell the nape of his neck and rub on his chest as he ignored me for the glow of his phone. He hopped off the bed.

"I'll be right back. I can't get a damn connection with this stupid WiFi box. You can take your shoes off. Make yourself comfortable. I'll be rightback."

James disappeared out the room and plodded down the stairs to the first floor. I was not about to be ignored for a WiFi connection. I decided to take things to another level.

“Which door is your bathroom?” I yelled down.

“If you’re in the room, it’s the first door to your left!” he yelled back at me.

I went into the bathroom to freshen up. Again, the bathroom was meticulously clean and everything matched. All of the assorted product bottles were lined perfectly down the sink, sorted by color and size. That was when I realized he didn’t have a girlfriend. He had OCD.

I slipped out of my clothes and got down to my bra and panties. I loved the way the black lace accented my rich brown skin. I was ready to go the distance. That’s when I heard it.

“Got it working! Yes!” James elated. The smooth sounds of Kenny G faintly played from his phone then suddenly got louder. I walked out of the room to see him sitting on the edge of the bed, playing with the music dock for his phone.

“Sorry about tha-” he started as he heard the door swing open. The sight of me in my bra and panties caught him off guard. He dropped whatever he was about to say. I straddled him on the edge of the bed and gave him a long, deep kiss. He gave no resistance as we fell backwards on the bed with me on top.

His big hands grabbed my bulging breasts as they popped out of the black lace. I pulled off my bra as we moved deeper and deeper into the fondling and caressing. Next, slipped off his T-shirt and grabbed his hard, pumped chest. We dry humped as things got heavy in a hurry. He slipped his pants off and threw them off the bed as I continued to attack him with kisses and grabs. It was exactly what I needed. He was standing at full attention. I felt his big hands reaching for my panties. I stopped him. It was too soon. Things were getting hot but we weren’t there yet.

“I just met you,” I whispered to him.

“I know,” he said.

He didn’t get the hint. I had to spell it out to him in between the kissing and touching. “Get a condom.”

He slid off the bed on command and went to the bathroom. He went through the medicine cabinet before reappearing and going through the drawers in his room.

“Let me run downstairs,” he said.

Not now,I thought. I didn’t want to wait for him to run to the store. I heard him rumbling through more cabinets and drawers. I laid back and closed my eyes to stay in the moment as Kenny G played softly from the dock.

Buzz! Buzz! Buzz!

My phone was going off. I reached down to pull it from my pants on the bedroom floor. It was Tricia calling. Crap. She thought I was still out with Justin. If I didn’t pick up, she was going to think something was wrong and blow my spot up. I had no choice. I picked up the phone and whispered into the speaker.

“Hello?”

“Girl, where are you? You said you’d call me when you get in!” Tricia yelled at me like she was my mother.

“I’m going home,” I said. She could read me too well. We’ve known each other far too long. She saw straight through the crap.

“Kate, *where are you? Who are you with?*” Tricia yelled back.

“I’m with a friend,” I said.

“Who?” she queried.

“You don’t know him,” I answered. “I’m alright, now chill.”

“Girl, you are over at a strange man’s house at this hour? *Where is Justin? What happened to the date?*” Tricia asked.

“Don’t worry about that,” I said. I could hear James still fumbling around downstairs and getting closer to the stairs. I tried to rush her off the phone. “I told you I’m fine. Let it go. I will talk to you later.”

“Kate, don’t do anything you are going to regret later. You said you wanted to go out with *your husband*,not some new piece of meat.”

I could hear James coming up the stairs. Tricia was right. This was wrong.

“Ok girl. I have to go.” I quickly hung up on her and grabbed my clothes. By the time James made it to the room, I was already fully dressed.

“What’s going on?” he asked. He was still empty handed, which meant this wasn’t going to work anyway. I realized what I was about to do. It finally hit me. My heart sank to the pit of my stomach. Who was I right now? Tears streamed down my face. How could I be so willing to break my vows so easily? I barely knew this man.

“I have a family emergency. I’m sorry. I have to go.” I ran down the stairs in a hurry and out the door. I quickly hopped in my car and pulled away from that huge mistake.

6

"Girl, what in God's green earth go into you?" Tricia asked as she sipped her mocha Frappuccino.

I decided to drive down to meet up with her at Starbucks. I badly needed someone to talk to. I sipped a tall Red Bull and thumbed through *O Magazine*. I know I looked a mess. My makeup was done quickly. My hair needed to be pressed and my work clothes were all wrinkled after the hour-long drive.

"I don't even know," I started. "Nothing even makes sense anymore."

"I mean, where did you meet this man?" Tricia asked.

"At a gas station," I replied. She rolled her eyes.

"Let me guess, was he white?" she asked.

"Yes," I confessed. "*And fine.* But that has nothing to do with it. I'm real weak right now. It's been *five months girl, five months!*"

"But you're married. You know you can't be going around in these streets like that!" Tricia snapped back at me. She was right. She always had a way of saying something in plain English that made perfect sense. "Besides, do you know what is in these streets? Stay married, girl."

"Wait, weren't you just warning me about going back to him?" I said.

"Yes. You can't forget what happened but if he has a mental illness, that's something you can work with him on. If he's getting treatment, that's completely different than when you didn't know he had problems," she responded.

"Wait, what? I lost you," I said.

"I'm saying if he has been diagnosed and knows how to control it, that's different than when you both had no idea what was going on," she said again.

"So you're saying I should go back? After one date?" I asked.

"No. I'm saying if you want to stay married, you BOTH now have PTSD. In sickness and health," she responded. "You getting your panties wet with some new man isn't going to change the fact that eventually, you have to face the decision of whether you want to deal with Justin's condition or not."

"I got you. But he was *so fine!* Sometimes in life you want to let go!" I said.

"Then get a divorce. You might as well have a clean break if you want to put your kitty cat in the streets like that!" Tricia yelled.

I was starting to get embarrassed. People in the Starbucks were eavesdropping and giving me weird looks. I grabbed Patricia by the arm and whispered loudly at her. "Why do you have to be so loud?"

"My bad, girl!" She smiled. "It's all love. You know that. I know you aren't trying to be in the streets like that. We all have needs, but yours should be tamed with some double A batteries while you're still legally married."

I sipped my Red Bull. "Girl you don't understand," I said. "He was so swole, strong and aggressive. He was such a *man*."

Tricia laughed at my excitement. "Well, did he at least eat the…"

"Oops! I showed up at the wrong time!" A familiar voice cut into the conversation. "But if that's on the menu, I'll put this coffee back." We looked up. It was Rashon.

Tricia laughed out loud as she stood to hug her friend. "You're so crazy!"

He joined us at our round table of gossip. "Hey, Kate."

"What's up?" I said to him.

"What did I walk in on?" Rashon asked.

"Wait, what are you doing here?" Tricia cut back.

"I come here to pick up beautiful women such as yourselves, of course," he joked. "I have some time to kill and I like to spend it people watching. I just walked in. What were ya'll up to?"

"We are having girl talk," I said.

"You want me to leave?" he asked as he pulled out his phone.

"You're fine," I said. It didn't matter at this point. He already knew I had issues.

Rashon browsed the internet on his phone as he continued. "So what's the dilemma? You can't find an extremely handsome single man to go out with tonight?"

Tricia cackled with laughter. "That would be easy in comparison."

Rashon grunted. He was in his own world. I decided to let him in since he was one of Tricia's close buddies and he kind of already knew me. "My husband has PTSD."

Rashon's head popped up. "You're married? I am going to need something stronger."

"Separated. There was an incident. I haven't decided if I should go back or not," I said.

"That explains a lot," he responded.

“Yeah… sorry about that. I didn’t know how to tell you,” I replied.

He popped his head back up from his phone. “All I know is that if you’re relying on this onefor relationship advice, something’s definitely wrong.”

“Hmmph.” Tricia grunted at him.

“Let’s be honest here. Patricia, you suck with relationship advice,” Rashon said. “You set me up with a married woman.”

I cut him off. “It’s ok. You shouldn’t have any problem with the ladies anyways. Don’t let me make you think anything’s wrong with you.”

“She likes white guys,” Tricia blurted out.

“Patricia!” I snapped at her.

Rashon threw his hands in the air. “See what I mean! Patricia, you’re the worst!”

“You’re a man. Let me ask your opinion on something,” Patricia said. “Would you mess with another woman if you were separated?”

Rashon looked at his phone for a minute as he thought about the question. He didn’t know what I was going through but I was on edge to hear his opinion regardless.

“By ‘mess with’, what exactly do you mean?” It was the typical man response.

“I mean all the way,” Tricia said. “Penetration!” People started looking at our table again. I was beginning to blush. Patricia couldn’t help but draw attention to us.

“That’s complicated,” he responded.

“That means yes,” I cut back at him.

He tried to clean up his answer. “I mean, separation is difficult. It depends on your relationship. It also depends on how much time has passed. If you’re totally cut off from your partner, I would think they’d expect you to eventually get it *somewhere.*”

Tricia blasted Rashon. “Don’t take her side. She isn’t going to let you hit!” Her volume now also embarrassed him.

“Ok ladies,” he said as he excused himself from the table with a big smile. “I’m going to get out of here before I catch a sexual harassment case.” He gave Tricia and me a quick hug before he disappeared.

***

“So that’s the deal,” my older lawyer said as she slid a document across the table in my direction. I had made the decision to consult with a divorce lawyer. I didn’t know if I was going to go through with it or not, but it had been six months and I was tired of waiting. A girl wanted to get back in the game, especially after the James incident. Tricia’s advice made a lot of sense. If I was going to do anything with anyone outside my marriage, the best idea would be to start with a clean break.

The lawyer was a nice white lady, about 55 years old with grayed hair and round Coke bottle glasses drawn across her neck by beads. I would imagine she’d been doing this for years. The quaint office displayed her advanced degrees in sociology, law, and criminal justice. Even though we had just met, there was probably a thing or two I could learn from Mrs. Powell.

“Since you two had no prenuptial agreements, you’d be entitled to spousal support. Considering he was discharged from the military and there’s a police report, this is an open and shut case.”

“I didn’t press charges though,” I said back to her quietly.

“Most victims don’t, especially when they are in a marriage. The courts already know that. You are still entitled to the spousal support since it was his actions that deemed the marriage unfit to continue,” she corrected me.

I didn’t like those terms. *Entitled, deemed.* This was my real life not some law book example. Taking what little money Justin had didn’t feel like the right thing to do. He was already on hard times.

She continued. “And you said there are no children?”

“None,” I replied. It hit me. If I went through with this, not only would it make Justin’s life horrible, the chances of us ever having children together would be over. I always talked about starting a family with him. How could I leave the marriage so soon? Was it my duty to try to see it that we have children? What if he wasn’t happy? Too many questions plagued my mind.

“He was diagnosed with Post-Traumatic Stress Disorder,” I confessed.

Mrs. Powell’s eyes lit up. She scribbled down some notes in her file. Mrs. Powell was old school. She handwrote everything before entering it in a computer.

“There are some precedents on this. You may be entitled to compensation from the US government. Very little people know about it, but there are certain funds that have set-asides for victims of war-related mental issues.”

“I don’t want to do that,” I said as I slouched back. The stress was starting to overcome me. Mrs. Powell was a pit bull, just as her Yelp reviews advertised but I was not interested in taking money I didn’t earn. I just wanted something that resembled my regular life back. I needed to get all of the uncertainty off my mind.

"What do you think?" I said.

"Think about what?" she responded. She wasn't sure if I was asking her as a woman or a client.

"I'm saying, if you were in my position what would you do?" I replied.

"I don't know. I'm not you. I can't predict what I would do if I were you," she answered.

I was not in the mood for lawyer talk. "Look. Can I ask you a question, woman to woman?" Mrs. Powell took her coke bottles off and peered at me.

"Sure. Shoot," she said.

"Do you like seeing people getting divorced? I know it's what you do for a living, but what do you feel about seeing them lose that person in their lives?" I said.

"There is nothing I can do about it," she said quickly. "I'm just the conduit to help someone do what they already want to do," she added.

"What do mean by that?" I said. I was so confused. This decision was really bearing on my thoughts.

"You seem to have a good reason to pursue this. Abuse is a real thing, but it's ultimately up to you what you want to do. Either you can break it off or you can stay in and see where it goes."

"That's the problem. I don't even know what the right move is," I said.

"Well. What do you want?" she asked me. Just as Tricia said, the ball was in my court.

“I just want to be free,” I said. “I just want to be with who I want to be with and be done with it.”

“Then what’s the problem? You came here, you’re clearly thinking about the divorce. It’s been six months.” Mrs. Powell said.

“You know what, I need more time. I need to talk to him about this,” I responded. “I’ll let you know in a week or so what I’m doing.”

I took the documents from her and left the office. It seemed surreal. There in my hands was the door out of my marriage if I wanted to take it. It wasn’t fair to make the ultimate decision without talking to Justin about it. I wanted him to know exactly what was up, for better or for worse.

***

That weekend, I decided to bite the bullet. I had to have *the talk* with Justin. I showed up at his friend’s house completely uninvited. I couldn’t get a hold of him on Facebook so I had to resort to extreme measure.

Justin’s car was parked outside. The Mustang was clean, as if he just washed it. I parked alongside the street and made my way to the front door. I took a big, deep breath and prepared to have one of the most difficult conversations of my life.

KNOCK. KNOCK. KNOCK.

I waited nervously at the door. Justin’s roommate opened the door. “Kate? I’m sorry, were never formally introduced.” He stuck his hand out. “I’m Gabe.”

“Nice to meet you. I’m sure you heard a lot about me.” I said. He dodged my comment.

"I'll tell Justin you're here. Come in." The house was nice but it was a typical man pad. None of the furniture matched, there was mail everywhere and football was playing on the television. I took a seat on one of the couches as I waited. I could hear them whispering in the back. A few seconds later Justin emerged from his room. He was still dressed in his pajamas.

"Kate?" I stood up to give him a hug. "What are you doing here?" he asked.

"It's nice to see you too," I responded. "We need to talk. I'd prefer not to do it here."

"About?" he asked. He was never one for surprises so I told him what was up. "About you, me, us. This. I spoke to a lawyer…"

I saw his heart drop. He looked as if he'd seen a ghost. "So you saw a lawyer. That's fine I guess. We can talk about it but there's really nothing to talk about. I understand what's coming," he said.

"Justin, please just get dressed," I said. He didn't respond as he left for his room. Minutes later, he reappeared in some slacks and a wrinkled T-shirt. He looked like he just learned Santa Claus didn't exist. It was tough to see him that disappointed.

We headed to a small café to sit and talk. I insisted that we drive separate cars. The whole situation was awkward and somber. It almost felt like a funeral.

Justin and I shared a small round table in the middle of the café. He bought himself a Red Bull and a Perrier water for me. This is not how I envisioned our lives going. Either way, I had to persist through it. I put the folder of documents on the table as he looked over them intently.

"So my lawyer says that I should incite abuse," I started. "But I don't think that's right." Justin said nothing as his cold blue eyes pierced the documents.

"No prenuptial agreement… request for spousal support?" he marked aloud as he read Mrs. Powell's notes. "Kate, who are you right now? Is this your idea or hers?"

"You told me to get a divorce," I said.

"Yes. If you wanted one," he corrected. "I don't even know what I'm reading. This isn't even your handwriting," he continued. "Cut the stuff, Kaitlyn. Is this how you feel or what you're being told you should feel by other people?"

"I just want to pursue my options. I can't stay separated forever. Life has to go on," I said. He let out a deep breath as he sat back in his chair.

"I don't think this is right. I don't think this is what you want. I don't believe it. I'm calling your bull. You don't want to do this."

I put my head in my hands and massaged my temples. I felt myself getting a headache. He grabbed my hands and held them softly. His eyes locked on mine. "Kate. What do *you* want?" he said.

"I just want it to be over," I said. "All this pressure, I can't deal with it. Every decision I make, I have to think what other people are going to say, what they want me to do."

"That's why I'm asking you what do *you* want?" he said. "If you want me to sign these papers, walk out of here and never speak to you again, I can do that."

"I barely speak to you now," I joked. "Are you going to un-friend me on Facebook too?"

“Only if you want me to,” he said. He was dead serious. For the first time in months, I heard conviction in his voice. My mind went blank. I leaned over the table, grabbed him by the cheeks, and planted my lips firmly on his.

He pulled back as he stared at me. The look in his eyes teetered between pain and infatuation. He drew his attention back to the papers. “So…?” he started.

I snatched the papers from him. “This is stupid,” I said.

7

"That's a three!" Gabe yelled at me and Justin. His foot was clearly on the line but I could tell he wasn't going to let it go. Gabe was a tanned, dark haired, short, skinny Marine. He was a second-generation Columbian-Venezulean but right now, he was a cheater in a game of 21.

Justin and I had decided to end our separation starting by doing regular activities together. He and Gabe invited me to the public basketball courts to shoot some hoops. The activity never mattered to me as long as Justin and I spent time together. His therapist advised that we hang out in group settings as we reestablished our relationship. Thus, Gabe was always the chaperone. Today he was a crooked referee as he headed to the free throw line, Spalding ball under his arm.

Justin jokingly yelled at him. "Your right foot was on the line! The whole foot! That was NOT a three."

"I don't know what you're talking about," Gabe said. "Kate, what did you see?" "Your foot was on the line," I said quickly.

"Ya'll are in it together. Just because that's your boyfriend doesn't mean you have to lie for him," Gabe said as he practiced his free throw form.

"Husband," I corrected.

"If you like it, you should put a ring on it!" Gabe joked as he strutted with the ball under arm, imitating Beyoncé.

Justin knocked the ball from under his arm. "Shoot your free throws, cheater. It doesn't matter. You're still going to lose." He was right. Justin was 6'4", I was 5'6", and Gabe was *maybe* 5'8".

Gabe's shot bricked. Justin got the rebound. I played defense on him. He backed me down using his backside for leverage. I grabbed him playfully but it didn't matter. He turned and sank his shot.

"Nineteen," he said as the shot went in. "And foul," he added.

"It's not a foul if you liked it," I laughed.

"Remember you said that," Gabe said.

"It's definitely a foul if you touch my ass, dude," Justin smacked back.

"You wouldn't be so lucky, honey," Gabe said as he snapped his fingers, imitating the mannerisms of a feminine gay man. Justin burst out laughing uncontrollably. He tried to contain himself to shoot the free throws.

The first shot went in. "Twenty," he said.

"No pressure," I said. If he made this next shot, Justin would win the game. The shot went up. It bricked off the backboard. He smacked his hands in disappointment. I got the rebound and dribbled around as Gabe defended me.

BANG! BANG! BANG!

A loud sound burst out of nowhere. It startled us. Some kid on another court was smacking his skateboard on the pavement. I looked at Justin. His eyes had that scary blank look. He crouched down on the blacktop quickly, as if he was going for cover. He was having a flashback. He was gone.

Gabe saw the fear in my face and immediately quit the game to tend to his friend. He grabbed Justin in a bear hug.

"Justin, it's ok! Snap out of it, dude! We're playing basketball."

Justin's eyes glazed over. It was that same lost look I saw during the previous incident. A few seconds later, he came back as he scanned his environment.

"I'm good. You can let me go," Justin said as he sat on the pavement, embarrassed. Gabe sat down next to him. I sat down on Justin's other side. He looked out at the kids, skating and shooting hoops.

"I'm sorry," Justin said.

I rubbed his back. "Don't worry about it. It's not your fault."

"You don't have to explain anything dude," Gabe added.

"You want to get out of here?" Justin said to me.

"Sure," I replied.

"I'm going to hang out a little while," Gabe said as he got up. I tossed him the ball. He took off towards the kids on the other court. I could hear him challenging them faintly in the distance.

Justin and I headed to his car. We pulled off the lot without exchanging a word. About five minutes later, he broke the silence. "I don't even know what happened…"

"You don't have to explain anything," I said. "It's not your fault."

"It was like I was back overseas. You don't even understand. It was so real. The sand, the mortars, I could see and hear it all," he said.

"I know." I really didn't, but I wanted to offer my support. We headed back to his and Gabe's place. I reeked of sweat and perspiration after the game. I badly wanted to get out of the workout clothes I had put on to meet them.

We headed inside. Justin got himself a glass of water. "You need anything?" he said in my direction.

"Yeah. I need to take a shower badly," I said. "I brought some clothes with me. They're in my car."

"Sure. You know where the bathroom is. Help yourself," Justin said as he gulped down the glass.

I ran out to my car and back inside to the bathroom. It felt like heaven to peel off my sticky, sweat-soaked clothes. I ran the shower with lukewarm water as I prepared to get in.

"Do you have any towels?" I yelled out to Justin.

"Yeah, they should be in there," he said back.

I looked back at the empty towel rack. He was wrong.

"I wouldn't ask you if there were some in here," I smartly said back.

"Ok. Let me get some from out the dryer," he responded.

A minute later, he knocked on the door. I was already fully undressed. He cracked the door open just enough to peek his hand and the towel through.

"You don't have to be like that. It's ok. We're married," I reminded him.

The door slowly opened. He looked like a child unwrapping his favorite toy on Christmas morning. He slowly scanned my body with his bright blue eyes. The smirk on his face was cunning and mysterious. He handed me the towel.

"Let me know if you need anything else," he said as I took the towel and placed it on the rack. I checked the water. Justin still hadn't left.

"What?" I said to him.

"Nothing," he answered.

"Now you're being weird," I said as I got in the shower. The water was finally just right, not too warm, not too cold. I pulled the shower curtain and ignored Justin.

Click. I heard the door shut as I lathered myself with body wash.

Standing in the shower beneath pulsing jets of hot water, I closed my eyes and massaged fragrant, soapy rivulets cascading down my body. As I turned, sapphire blue eyes peered through a misty gap that widened as hands wiped a clear patch, reflecting the leering smile on a handsomely chiseled face.

I responded by tweaking my bullet-hard nipples. "Justin, if you were a dog you'd be drooling by now."

"I am a dog, Kate," he said, quickly stepping out of his T-shirt and jeans. "Woof."

Now it was my turn to leer. Justin's well cut body was eye candy for any red-blooded female, but his truncheon-hard shaft rising like a fleshy flagpole was more invitation than I could resist.

"I guess that redefines the meaning of throw the dog a bone," I said, "or should I say, boner?"

Laughing, Justin opened the shower door and stepped into my waiting arms. We melted into a passionate embrace, our lips locking into deep kiss. As our tongues fenced, we descended to the floor, our slippery bodies writhing in the foamy water.

"Since I'm behaving like a dog today," he said huskily, "then we're going to have to do it doggy style."

Justin knelt behind me and pushed me onto my hands and knees, then spread my ass wide beneath the pulsing spray. Water pooled on my back and dripped down my smooth crack, trickling onto my swollen, pink lips. I gasped when I felt his probing fingers tease my engorged lips. Raising my hips, I whimpered and ground my ass against his face, my hands scrabbling to grip the slick floor.

Now his tongue snaked into my hot, sticky crevices and hungrily lapped at my hole. Jolts of pleasure shot through my body like electrical currents. My eyes tightly shut, I began to violently thrust against him even before he roughly gripped my hips and impaled me with his rigid shaft. With a grunt, he began pumping me fast and hard. His thick meat stretched me, his manhood slapping against my thighs. I was so wet I could hear my juice slurping. Our cries echoed as we bucked in frenetic rhythm. My thighs trembled, my breasts slapped furiously against the tile. Already hot from the shower, I began to feel almost faint from the tension building in my core. Justin's left hand trailed down from my hip, his fingers teasing the tight ring of my ass, which quivered expectantly at his touch.

Slicking his fingers with the juice leaking from my hole, he inserted three deep inside me. I screamed and jerked so violently I almost knocked him off balance, but he clutched me tightly, working both my holes until the aching pressure from my impending climax finally exploded like a tsunami crashing ashore. I screamed as wave after wave of intense pleasure spasmed throughout my body. My strangled cries melded with his, his spurting shaft violently jerking inside me. Exhausted, spent, we collapsed into each other's arms on the floor.

Thump. Thump. I heard the sound of the front door opening and closing. Gabe was back. I looked at Justin and mouthed the words to him. "Get out. Hurry up!"

"YOOOO!" Gabe yelled from the living room. Justin shrugged.

"Yoooo!" he yelled back.

"Go. Go. Go," I mouthed to him. He threw on his shorts and popped out of the bathroom.

"What's up?" he said to Gabe.

"Where's Kate?" Gabe asked in response.

"She's changing," Justin answered. I got myself together and came out of the bathroom a few minutes later.

"Somebody had sex baby! Let's talk about you and me!" Gabe sang as he mocked the 90's song.

"No we didn't," I said. "And if we did, it's not a big deal."

"Married couples don't have sex. You know that," Justin said, laughing.

"I had sex once," Gabe said. "You two should try it. It's pretty awesome," he joked. We all laughed.

***

Over the next few weeks, Justin and I got back to what seemed like normal.

I would spend as much time as possible with him and Gabe while trying not to invade their spot. Gabe was extremely supportive. He didn't seem to care I was over so much. Though we stayed in separate places, we were together almost daily. He still did not know where I lived, though I did tell him that I was living in the same complex.

Justin's money situation improved as his depression went away. He started looking for better jobs than the Burger Shack, but there were only so many options for someone who was so villainously discharged. One day, he came to me with an idea that was a bit shaky. We sat around their dinner table, which was littered with various pieces of mail, *Maxim* and *ESPN* magazines.

"Kate, what do you think about this?" Justin said as he handed me his iPad. On the screen was a Realtor.com listing. It was a beautiful condo, not too far from where we used to live together. Obviously, this was his way of saying we should move back in together. We had just crossed the bridge of going out socially alone.

"What are you thinking?" I asked.

"I'm just seeing if you like it," he said as he half smiled.

"It's a nice condo. Good location. A bit pricey though," I said.

"What do you think about looking at places?" he asked. His eyes longed for a response that agreed with the notion.

"Looking can't hurt," I responded.

I swiped through a few listings on the iPad. Nothing particularly interested me. I already had my own place and was locked into my lease for a few more months. I knew we had to consider moving back in together eventually though.

"These places are really high," I said. "I'm not sure we could even afford anything on here. And besides, what has your therapist said about moving back in together?"

His eyes lit up. He smiled. "Therapy is going perfect. No issues. I'm fine to resume my, our, normal life."

"Oh is that right?" I teased. "*Everything* hasn't resumed to normal," I said knowingly.

"Why do you have to be such a perv?" Justin joked back. "Everything takes time. And besides, I don't like Gabe around when we do that. This is precisely why we need our own place."

He was right but I wasn't ready to cross that bridge. We weren't even getting intimate often. Why push to move back in so quickly?

"We need a plan," I said. "If this is going to work, obviously things have to change. First of all, is figuring out how we're supposed to afford these prices." I continued to swipe through the listings. Each place was more expensive than the pervious.

"I agree," Justin said. "I just don't know what to do. That discharge may as well be a felony."

"Do you remember when we first met?" I asked. It was time to change the topic to something a lot more positive.

"Yes. How could I not remember?" he said. "I was such a nerd. I couldn't even talk to you."

"Oh really?" I teased. "This is new news. Please continue."

"You don't know. You are intimidating," He answered.

"I am?" I questioned.

"Well, not you… black girls in general. You know the stereotype."

"Ahh, I see." I replied. "Continue."

"Let me paint the picture," he started. He wiped his unmanaged hair out of his face as he recollected. "I'm out with my military buddies and we're bar hopping. We went up and down Front Street, harassing women all night. That's what we were good at, getting drunk and antagonizing women." He laughed as he continued. I perked up. I had never heard this story in detail.

"So we go to one spot and it's dead, all soccer moms on an extended happy hour. No one's trying to hop on a grenade just yet. It was still early in the night, so we go to another place, that little Irish Pub. You know the spot."

I nodded as I smiled at the grenade comment. He went on. "So we're in the Pub and it's alright but it's a sausage fest. Way too many drunk Marines were already in there. There were a few girls, all white girls mind you, but everyone was talking to them. One after another, guy-after-guy, rejection. It was ugly. I remember thinking at that moment, what was I doing with my life? I was twenty-four and chasing skirts like I was still seventeen. Eventually you have to snap out of it. That was my epiphany as I saw each one of my boys, Stevenson, Paulson, and Davis, all do the same shit: walk up to a girl, say something stupid and wait for her to either reject you or realize she's just drunk enough to take home."

I cut my eyes sharply at him. I was not privy to these drunken hook-ups nor was I trying to have that mental picture.

"So we all get rejected there and it's like midnight. Midnight and we already blew out two spots. I had enough but we went to one last place…"

"Justin, where do I come in this story?" I cut in. I knew how the story ended but I was not trying to hear how I was girl number seventy-three in the night.

"I'm getting there, babe," he said. "So we're on our way to one last spot and Paulson's crying. He won't shut up. He has a headache."

I chuckled. I knew exactly where this story was going. He kept going. "We're like, Paulson you can get a cab and go back to the barracks by yourself because we're not going home without talking to some girls. So we walk to CVS and bam! There you and your friends were."

A huge smile painted my face as he finished the story. "But the issue was that we could tell you weren't going to go for the drunk approach. So I, as the sober one, said screw it and spoke."

"I believe I spoke to you first," I said. "I know for a fact I did. I asked you what you were doing."

"Well, that's the story," he finished. "But what was your point?"

"We made it work. Even though it was awkward and uncomfortable at first, we kept at it," I said.

"True," he answered. "Those were the good old days," he reminisced.

"And I'm still here," I said as I glanced over more listings on the iPad. "If this is going to work, we have to continue to work together. Even when no one thinks it can work."

He snapped back to the original topic. "What's up with your place?"

"What do you mean?" I asked.

"Your place. I know you aren't comfortable with the idea yet but why not just live back there?"

"That's too close to… the past," I answered.

"You're right. I just want to get our own spot again. I need to find a better job," he said as he thumbed through a *Maxim*. He gave up on the thought as he excused himself from the table and threw the magazine back on the pile of paper.

BUZZ!

An alert went off on the iPad. Justin's attention was elsewhere and he didn't notice.

It read: *SANDRA*

HEY! ARE WE STILL ON?

CAN'T WAIT! ☺

My heart exploded in my chest.

Who the fuck was Sandra?

8

The next day, work went by in a haze. I don't remember what I did that day because the entire time my mind was locked on one thing. *Sandra.* When it came time to go for the day, I left in a hurry and without greeting any of my coworkers. I drove home as fast as possible in anticipation of the night's Facebook investigation.

I scoured Facebook for hours. I typed in every variation of Sandra I could think of. *Who was this and what couldn't she wait for?* My blood boiled as I thought of just the *idea* of another woman. I searched page after page, profile after profile, trying to find out who was it that texted Justin.

His friends list had no Sandra listed and there were no out of place comments. All his photos were of himself, his car, or me. I could not piece together what was going on. If there was another chick then he was real slick, having photos of me on the page. I couldn't find anything off about his page. Thankfully, he was offline at the time.

There were like 35 *Sandra's* in our area and none of them were cute, at least I thought not. Most of them were either too young or too old to be the woman in question, but that didn't mean anything. I knew that people could hide their profiles.

Buzz! Buzz! Buzz!

My phone went off in the other room. I ignored it. This was more important. If it was Justin, I didn't want to speak to him anyway. The Facebook investigation went deeper and deeper as I searched the friends of the Burger Shack's page just to make sure this chick didn't work with him.

KNOCK. KNOCK. KNOCK. KNOCK!

Someone was at my door. I wasn't expecting any visitors today. It couldn't be Justin because he didn't know what number my place was and I always parked a building over just in case. I wondered who it could be as they knocked relentlessly.

I got up and grabbed a butcher's knife from the kitchen as I tiptoed towards the door. If it was a criminal, he was going to get the surprise of his night. I looked through the peephole. It was Tricia. She knocked again. She wasn't going to give up.

I opened the door.

"What do you want?" I said.

"Nice to see you too," she said as she slid her big butt past me and into my apartment. She had a way of making whatever place she was at hers. "Girl I got to go!" she said as she kicked off her shoes and ran barefoot to the bathroom. That was about as close of a greeting I was going to get out of her. I put the knife back.

"What are you doing here?" I yelled at Tricia as she made herself comfortable in the bathroom.

"It's an emergency! I had to come back you up ASAP, girl! Soon as I got your text I had to make my way."

"I appreciate it," I said. The water ran then shut off. She reappeared from the bathroom.

"So who is this bitch Sandra?" she began.

"No idea," I answered. I plopped down on the loveseat of my little one bedroom apartment. Tricia sat at my round dining table as she checked her phone.

"So tell me the story again. How did you find out about this?" she asked.

"I was using his iPad and the message came on the screen," I said.

"But he doesn't even have a phone," she replied.

"That's what I thought but apparently, he has iMessage," I said.

"And you don't have iMessage?" she asked.

"No. I have a Droid. But that's beside the point." I got up to get my laptop from my room. I placed it on the round table with Tricia.

"Look," I said as I pointed to the listings of Sandras. "All these Sandras and none of them are on his friends list."

"That doesn't mean anything," she replied as she pushed her new perm out of her eyesight. "Men are all the same. Social networks just make it that much easier for them to do something slick."

I wasn't trying to hear it. This was not the same. I snapped at her. "Tricia, I am married! This is not the same."

"*Legally,*" she emphasized. "Ya'll don't act married. Ya'll live in two different places. You don't have phone communication. And ya'll are not even having sex." I got up from the table without a word.

"You want something to drink?' I asked.

"Kaitlyn!" she screamed at me. I dug my head in the fridge.

"I got Perrier water, Red Bull, Peach Ciroc…"

Tricia yelled at me with even more emphasis. "KAITLYN!"

"*What?*" I spat back.

"When did you let him back in?" she asked.

I explained myself. "It just happened. Just a couple times. Stop being like that. I am *married* after all."

“Legally,” she dismissed. “Now that he has what he wants, what makes you think he’s going to do the right thing?” I poured myself a glass of the Ciroc.

“He wants to move back in together,” I said as I rejoined the table.

“I don’t think that’s a good idea,” Tricia said.

“Why? Because of the message? The therapy is about over. They actually advised to work on getting back to our regular lives.” She kept clicking through Facebook screens.

“Not because of that,” Tricia said as her eyes widened. She spun the laptop to my view.“Because of THIS.”

***

I sped down the highway with tears in my eyes. How could I be so dumb? How could I not see this?

I got to his place so fast I didn't even remember parking the car. I was suddenly at the door pounding on it, demanding my answers. Justin answered the door with an unworthy innocent look on his face. I wasn't going for it. I shoved the printed photo in his face.

"What is this!" I screamed at him. He was bewildered by the sneak attack.

"What are you talking about, Kate? Calm down!" he commanded.

"Look at the photo! Tell me that isn't you!" I yelled back.

He took the paper from my hands and inspected it. His eyes pierced through each pixel. He was caught red handed, but he wasn't going to go down that easy.

"Kate, where did you get this from?" he asked sternly.

"Don't ask me where I got it from!" I screamed. "Tell me what it is!"

"I'm getting to that. Where did you get this? What are you doing snooping around my friends' Facebook accounts!" he retorted.

I mushed him in the face. "What is this!"

He stepped back from the doorway and took a moment to process what was happening. I tried to catch my breath as I waited to hear his explanation.

"Kate. Just leave it alone." he said. What? This was his explanation?

"Leave it alone?" I questioned. "Leave what alone? Tell me what's going on!" My blood boiled as he got quieter and quieter. That's when I totally blacked.

"Who is Sandra? Who in the hell is Sandra!" I snapped as I rushed him. I slapped him in the face repeatedly as he said nothing. My soul burned as I beat my pain into his face. I didn't care anymore. Nothing mattered except inflicting as much pain as humanly possible.

WHACK!

My head snapped back as he retaliated with aggression. That blank look overtook his face. My heart stopped. He knocked me to the floor with a haymaker and kept coming. He grabbed me. I kicked, clawed and scratched to break free as we exchanged blows. I was again terribly overmatched. The familiar taste of my own blood filled my mouth.

He said nothing as he viciously attacked me. I ran through the kitchen, looking for a butcher knife. Nothing. That's when I suddenly remembered that I brought my pistol with me just in case this exact scenario went down. I reached for my back pocket and there it was. I pulled the Beretta and aimed it at his chest.

"Not another move," I said. "This is where this ends."

He kept coming and coming. I had to pull the trigger.

BANG!

Justin was no more.

***

BEEP! BEEP! BEEP!

The dim from the red LED numbers slowly came into focus. 6:30 AM.

I rolled across the bed as everything slowly came into focus. The dim from the laptop illuminated my bedroom. It was just a dream. Sadly, the photo on my laptop screen was still very real.

Work went by in another haze. I had no idea how I was getting anything done. For the past few weeks, everything was on autopilot at the workplace. I was in the routine of coming in, working at my desk and leaving without saying a word to a soul. It was unhealthy, but my mind was totally preoccupied with what I had to deal with after work.

I decided it was best to just deal with it head on. Immediately after work, I drove over to Justin's place. Taking heed to the premonition from the previous night, I brought a pocket mace with me just in case things got out of hand.

I took a deep breath as I knocked on the door.

Justin answered the door. He was happy to see me. "Hey babe, what's up?" He said with a big smile and hug. I entered the home calmly as I sat my purse on the kitchen table.

"We have to talk about something," I said sternly. Justin was taken aback by the tone.

"Ok. What's up?" he said as he joined me at the table.

"I'm going to ask you something and I need a 100% honest answer," I started as I pulled the printed photo from my purse. "Who is this and why is someone named Sandra texting you?"

The photo was of him and some brunette chick, cheek to cheek with the caption "Love this guy!" The look in Justin's eyes said it all. He was caught. He cocked his head back and let out a deep breath. "Look, Kate…"

"Don't 'look, Kate' me. Answer the question, Justin. Why did I have to find out about this on Facebook? If you have someone else, just let me know so I can quit wasting my time and energy on this marriage."

"Kate, calm down," he said quietly. "I don't even know how you saw that. I would never disrespect you. You're my wife and…"

I cut him off. "Answer the question. Who is Sandra, Justin?"

"She's just a girl," he said.

"And?" I snapped back. "This photo doesn't say just a girl."

"We were together about four months after we separated. It never went anywhere," he confessed. His voice was sincere as his eyes started to water. "That's it. She's no one."

"Justin, did you… are you f'ing this girl? Just tell me. Don't waste my time," I said.

"No!" he answered immediately. "I don't even talk to her like that. We were together two times. She went down on me. Nothing else happened. It never went further than that. I swear on my life."

I took a moment to process everything. One part of me was pissed he could do such a thing, but the guilt from my own indiscretions told me to let it go. I could deal with this.

"So why does the caption say I love this guy?" I continued.

"That picture is not hers. It's from Paulson's page, and you know that. I met her through the group. She works with Davis' wife. I wasn't out here trying to pick up random women if that's what you're getting at."

Everything sounded fair enough except for iMessage. "Why is she texting you?" I said.

"I originally got that iPad for *you*," Justin remarked. "So you could watch Netflix, don't you remember that? I was with her and Davis when I got it and they set up the iMessage for me. It's the only way I can text the whole group. If you saw anything, it was a group message. Do you really think I'd hand you my iPad if I had other chicks texting me? Come on Kate, I'm not that dumb."

I thought about it. Everything seemed to make sense. A load was taken off. The best part of all, I didn't have to mace Justin. I got up from the table. I was still in my work clothes. "I don't want you texting her. If we're going to be moving in together, it's not going to work if you're texting Sally Sue."

Justin wiped his forehead and sighed. "I messed up. I'm sorry. Let me make it up to you."

"Don't apologize; just don't let it happen again," I said as I walked out.

9

"$3000 for a table!" Justin remarked.

Tricia and I ignored him as we unbuttoned our coats and made ourselves comfortable. We were on a group excursion to the local Furniture Depot to look at home furnishings. I thought it would be a good idea to reintroduce Justin slowly back into my regular social life. Tricia was cool with it, although Justin was still nervous about being around my ace.

"But it's hand carved mahogany, babe!" I whined in my best girly voice.

Justin was still at Burger Shack so this table was clearly out of the question, although the dark chocolate brown finish on it was incredible. Justin was always the type to have sticker shock. Tricia teased him to no end about it.

"Sit down, Justin. Join us at the dinner table, my lad," she said with her best fake British accent.

Justin obliged. Tricia grilled him in the English accent. "So when are we moving back in together, mate?" she asked. "And when are we taking this table with us?" Justin laughed.

"Did you just switch to an Australian accent? And you have to ask your friend when we are moving back in together," he said, pointing toward me.

"Soon enough," I said, which was an honest answer. It was time. It had been over seven months since the incident. Things were going great. There was no reason to delay it other than money.

I got up from the table as we continued to walk the furniture warehouse. We came over to a nice bedroom display. It had a beautiful Queen sized bed with a nice dark brown headboard and bedposts, complete with matching burgundy sheets and rugs. I plopped down on the bed.

Tricia and Justin walked around the edge of the bed, admiring the details of the wood. Justin, of course, found the sticker price.

"$9000!" he said loudly. "For $9000, I'm thinking it better come with another wife to keep me warm when you get tired of me."

I laughed. "Nope. You better pick out a nice loveseat because that's where you'll be when that happens."

Tricia excused herself. "I'm getting tired. I'll meet you two outside. I'm going to get me something to drink." She left for the Italian Ice shop next door. Justin joined me on the luxurious bedding.

"I wish I could give you all this," he said. "You deserve the world for giving me another chance and doing everything you've done to make this work. Even forgiving me for San-"

I cut him off. I grabbed his face and pulled him in a deep, warm kiss. We fell back on the enchanting, soft bedding as if it was our own home.

We made out like two little teenagers madly in love in the near empty warehouse. There were a few employees going about but they paid no mind as Justin and I made ourselves at home. Hands went everywhere from squeezing bulging pockets of flesh to slipping a hand underneath and getting a warm up. One of the employee's sudden voices compelled us stop the make out session.

"I got a delivery. You want me to handle it now?" a boisterous familiar voice shouted across the warehouse. That's when I saw the beautiful stranger. James. He was working the delivery truck. The hair stood up on the back of my neck. My heart pounded uncontrollably. My palms itched. I had to figure something out as he began approaching our direction.

James trotted towards us in his usual blue-collar get up of steel toe boots, jeans and a dark wool coat. He still wore that scruffy five o'clock and his long hair was even longer and messier now. I had to think of something.

Think, Kate. Think, Kate.

My eyes grew wider with each pace. I grabbed Justin by the back of the neck and turned our faces down as James approached.

"Babe, see if you can find the price on this rug," I said quietly so James wouldn't hear my voice.

Tap. Tap. Tap.

He walked right by as my body temperature grew with each pace. Finally, we were in the clear as he passed us. I peeked back to make sure he was out of sight and grabbed Justin to get out of there.

"Forget it. We can't afford anything here. We should have gone to the flea market. Let's find Tricia and get out of here," I said as I led Justin at a brisk pace out of the furniture depot.

We found Tricia in the Italian Ice shop, sipping on lemonade and talking to one of the workers. He was a tall, dark, Italian guy who seemed to grow a liking to her. I could tell by the look in his eye he was interested on taking Tricia's full figure for a ride, but we had bigger issues. I didn't want to cockblock but we had to get moving.

"Tricia!" I said in my best fake happy voice. "Are you ready?"

She responded. "Not yet. Kate, this is…"

I cut her off before I could get his name. "Nice to meet you. Tricia, I thought you said you were tired?" I signaled to her in my best girl code voice that we had a code red.

“I’m fine now. You don’t have to rush for me. *I think I can find something to do,*” she said as she eyeballed her Italian stallion.

Justin remained quiet as he dabbled at the menu. There was no time for icees or quickies. I had to get out of here as soon as possible. I grabbed Tricia’s lemonade and headed for the door. “Sorry about the rush but we have to go,” I said with no explanation.

When we got out in the parking lot, my body ached once more. Immediately next to the Mustang was the Furniture Depot truck with the receiving gate lifted. I could see James’ messy mop of hair bobbing around in the back of the truck. There was no way to get to the car.

“On second thought, I want an icee. You want an ice, Justin? Come on, Tricia, my treat. That was rude of me.” I turned immediately around and led them back to the icee shop.

“You’re acting weird,” Justin said. “You usually aren’t this indecisive.”

“I guess my sweet tooth is finally catching up with me,” I replied.

***

“Are you serious!” Rashon laughed as he threw his hands up. I needed to talk to someone and I trusted him enough to talk to him. I promised him dinner on me if he met up. We met at a Starbucks halfway between both of us.

“Yeah, that’s exactly how it went down,” I said. “I just turned and there he was. I’m so lucky nothing happened. Tricia doesn’t even know what happened yet.”

“She’s going to flip out,” Rashon said. “What are you getting?” he asked as he turned his attention to the counter.

"I'm going to get a decaf green tea," I answered on autopilot.

"Nah, you got to try that raspberry iced tea," Rashon corrected. He was dressed up in a brown jacket with a white button down and dark jeans. As usual, he was on the prowl.

"What are you getting?" I asked back.

"Since you're buying, I'm about to get that Turkey Panini," he said with a big Kool-Aid smile.

"By the way, this doesn't count as our second date," I said. "Just in case you're counting."

"Aight, aight, cool," he said. "Don't be so crazy about it. Now back to the dilemma. What are you going to do?"

"I think it's best if I don't say anything. As a man, what is your honest opinion? Would you want to know if you were Justin?" I asked.

"Want to know everything? Nah, but you can at least tell him about the other guy. At least make it less sneaky." He shrugged his shoulders as if to say *that's all I got*. I sighed.

"What he doesn't know cannot hurt him, right?" I said.

"If you say so." He got up to order his sandwich and our drinks. "I'm craving that turkey."

A minute later, Rashon rejoined me. "You gotta tell him if you think it's going to come up. Is he a jealous type of guy?"

"No," I answered. "He's pretty laid back. I'm just afraid of triggering anything. You know, the PTSD and all…" Rashon made a concerned face as he responded.

"Totally forgot about that." He thought for a moment. "I still think you should tell him. Just tell him there's a guy you met when you separated that might call you and he shouldn't be threatened about it."

I thought about it. It made sense but it was still risky. Rashon continued. "And you should tell him that man is me." I laughed at his nerdy sense of humor.

"You're stupid," I said back. "Here is the part you don't know. There is another girl somewhere on the side."

His eyes lit up. "Another girl?Kate, I didn't know you were in to that. Do tell more." I slapped him on the forearm.

"No! Not like that. When we separated, he had a girl on the side. So it goes both ways."

"And how did you find out about it?" he asked.

"Group text. He claims he didn't bang her though. She just went down on him. He claims."

Rashon's big bushy eyebrows arched up. "I don't know. That sounds suspicious to be honest. But if he's going to tell you that happened, then why wouldn't he tell you he went all the way?"

I took it in. "You're right. He's probably telling the truth. But still, no woman wants to hear that." This was the real conversation I needed to have.

"How did he meet this girl?" Rashon asked.

"Through one of his buddies. What do you think about that?" I said.

"Sounds like a layup." he said dismissively.

"Layup? What's that? I'm not privy to this slang," I said.

Rashon corrected me. “You’re not privy to brothers.”

I snapped back. “Here we go.Would it make you happy if I threw the box at the next brother I see?”

He chuckled. “I’m the only one here. I won’t judge you.”

For a moment, he actually had a little swagger.

He flashed a big knowing smile. “You know I’m right. Someone’s got to bring you back to the dark side. Anyways, back to the point. A layup is a girl you don’t have to work for. If his boys put him on the girl then it’s almost offensive if he doesn’t take the layup. It’s an unwritten guy code.”

I didn’t want to hear more. “Get our drinks,” I told him. I went to the counter with him to pay as he grabbed the drinks and sandwich. We sat back at the table.

“What’s new in your world? Still single, I’m guessing?” I asked.

“Of course,” he said bluntly.

“What do you mean by that?” I snapped back.

“It’s hard out here for the brothers. You wouldn’t understand.”

I smirked at the comment. “Oh really? Do tell.”

He began on what felt like a softly rehearsed tirade on his dating experience.

“First of all, it’s hard enough being a single man in this society. With all the gender roles reversed and crap, you have a lot of women that don’t even *want* a man. And don’t get me started on the ones that don’t want to date the brothers. Combine all of that into a cocktail of desperation and that’s basically my life.”

For a moment, I almost felt sorry for him.

"Look at you." I said. "The problem is you're looking for someone. You can't let people set you up, especially people like Tricia because they don't know any better. When you're least expecting it, you'll find someone."

The comment visibly disturbed him.

"You know who else told me that? My mother, when I was 12. I'm 27 now and have never had anything serious in the relationship department. Meanwhile, all my buddies have married their college sweethearts and are having children. But it's whatever. You're probably right."

I actually felt sorry for him after hearing that.

"I didn't mean anything by that. I just mean, well, you're a nice guy. Look at you dressed all up. You mean to tell me you've never had any serious girlfriends? I don't believe that."

He laughed. "You never know when Halle Berry is going to show up. I stay fly so I don't have to get fly. But to answer your question, there is one girl. I don't have time to tell you the whole story but I'll give you the cliff notes. I met her in college but I was horribly under-socialized because I was a blerd."

I stopped him. "Blerd?" I asked.

"Black nerd. Like Childish Gambino," he replied, to which I gave him the *I dunno* look.

"Steve Urkel. But before he realized he could be Stephon." I nodded as I got the reference.

He continued.

"Anyways, my homies knew I liked her and they would literally call her *my girl*. She was beautiful too. Tall, light skin, long black hair, nice smile, pleasant attitude, everything I was looking for. So they set me up with her and I just blew it. I effing blew it." He shook his head in disgust.

"You have to elaborate." I said.

"Well my homie sets the meeting up or whatever and we are sitting at the table, me and her. She's 12 inches away from my face and I can't say anything. My body literally could not make sound. I just froze up thinking about not messing it up. Then she gave me her number, I guess out of pity, and I never called because I thought she was out of my league."

I nodded as I followed the story. I offered a word of encouragement. "That's understandable. That happens all the time with shy guys…"

He stopped me. "Oh no, Kate. There is more. The story gets worse. So it happens a year later, again. It's the same exact scenario with the same girl. My homie sets it up and I freeze up and blow it, AGAIN. And she gives me her number and I don't call. *Again*."

I cringed. "Ouch."

He went on. "Ouch indeed. And it gets even more awkward. That haunts me every day for years until I finally get the nerve to holler at her again… via Facebook."

I cringed even harder. "And she didn't reply?"

He shook his head in disappointment. "Of course not. But now you know more about me and why I'm so awkward."

I grabbed him by the hand. His touch was warm and gentle. "Listen Rashon, you are a really good guy. You are going to make someone really happy one day. Don't beat yourself up about the past. There's nothing you can do about it. If she was smart, she would have snatched you up by now. If it's going to happen, you have to let the universe work. You'll find what you're looking for. Don't sweat it."

"So what's the next move for you?" Rashon asked as he devoured what was left of his Panini.

I clasped my head in my hands. "We are supposed to be moving in together soon."

"When?"

"Soon," I said.

"How soon is soon?" he asked.

"Weeks, days," I said. "I just hope no drama happens. I probably need to change my phone number while I'm thinking about it."

"My honest advice is that you put everything on the table before you move in together. He sounds like a stand up guy. Just tell him and let him deal with it. If you think anything is going to trigger, then try to do it in public," he said as he washed down the Panini with his iced tea. It was great insight into a man's mind but my mind was made up.

I was going to take my chances and not say anything.

10

Two weeks later, almost 8 months to the exact day we separated, Justin and I moved back in together. Justin hauled in his things in two cardboard boxes. I reluctantly agreed to let him move in my new apartment since the lease was already signed. He hadn't had any episodes and everything was fine according to therapy. It was time to get our lives back on track.

"Do you need help with anything?" I asked as he brought in the second large brown box.

"That's everything," he responded.

"That's two boxes. All your stuff fit in those two boxes?" I asked.

"Of course. I'm a man. We don't carry baggage everywhere," he said as he sat down on one of the boxes holding his belongings. He was taking it in. The look on his face said it all. It was finally over.

"Kate?" he asked.

"What?" I replied.

"I just realized, you have like no furniture."

It was true. All I had was one couch, the small round dining table, my bed, and a dresser.

"Well this place is pretty small," I said to my defense. "Do you want something to drink?"

"You know I'm not drinking right now," he said.

"We need to celebrate. Take a load off," I encouraged. I got two glasses and poured some Ciroc for us. I handed Justin a glass and sat on the floor next to his boxes.

"No TV?" he asked.

"Nope," I replied. "No time."

He looked at me as if I had three heads. "So what do you do to pass time?"

I confessed. "Facebook, or talk to my friends. I never watched a lot of TV, you know that."

"So we need to get a TV," he said with his hand on his chin.

"We don't really need a TV. Why can't you live without TV?" I asked.

"I need to watch the news," he responded in a matter-of-fact way.

"Well for now, we can entertain each other." I said.

"Doing what?" He smiled.

I grinned. "I don't know but I'm sure we can find something."

He slid off the box and joined me on the floor. A devilish grin was on his face. He grabbed me without saying a word.

Without saying a word, Justin pulled me into an embrace. We fell against the boxes stacked around us and impatiently pushed them away. Though the unheated apartment was chilly, once his hands started roaming under my sweater and cupped my breasts, warmth quickly transformed into slowly simmering heat.

"No bra … again?" Justin asked, cocking an eyebrow.

I grinned innocently. "They were all in the laundry. You know how that goes."

His hands trailed toward my jeans and unzipped them, his questing fingers soon discovering my naked ass. He clucked at me with mock disapproval.

"And your panties are all in the laundry as well, I suppose?"

“Who needs panties when I’m not going be wearing them in a moment?” I said, pushing him onto his back. Unzipping his jeans, his stiff member eagerly sprang into my hands.
Justin closed his eyes, then jerked and moaned as I trailed my hands down the quivering length of his member and caressed his taut extremities. I loved the feel of his warm flesh against my fingers and the way it responded to my touch. Justin was huge, a good eight inches, but there were times when he became so aroused his pole swelled even larger and would really stretch me.
Guiding his pole into my hot mouth, I trailed my tongue around the glans and gently lapped at a pearly bead of his juice, which tasted both sweet and salty. Justin shivered and muttered obscenities under his breath, his body tensing. When I abruptly swallowed him down to his manhood, he cried out and clawed at the carpet.
The room became unbearably hot, and I felt a sheen of sweat erupt on my body. We paused the action long enough to strip out of our clothes. My sticky juice oozed from my hole and trailed down my thighs, and I ached to feel Justin slide inside me.
Kneeling between his legs, I began to slowly lick and suck his shaft, my head rising and falling like a piston. I felt his distended veins in my mouth, his extremities tightening in my hand until they felt like the knobby texture of an orange skin.
Brushing damp strands of hair from my face, I pulled him from my mouth and squeezed his member between my breasts. Justin groaned from the unexpected switch, but the ecstatic expression on his face as I buried his meat deep into my cleavage was worth it. I could tell by the way his extremities were tightening that he was about to explode all over me, so I quickly rose and straddled him.
My box was so swollen and sensitized I gasped from the contact of his shaft as it slipped into my juicy hole. Justin and I both moaned as he thrust deep and hard. Clasping hands, we rocked in frantic rhythm for only a few moments before we simultaneously came, our spasms merging into a primal cry.
Drained, I collapsed into his arms, our hearts beating together as one.

***

“You should call Gabe and see if he wants to come too,” I said as I ransacked my closet, looking for the correct blouse to match with my tan heels. Justin and I had decided to get together with our friends for a big dinner, and everyone was invited. It was part of the whole "get out lives back to normal" movement forward.

I invited Tricia and Rashon, along with Justin's friend Davis and his wife, to join us for dinner at a PF Chang's restaurant. It was the first time we had put a dinner group together in over a year. We usually tried to have a big dinner at least once a month to keep everyone in the loop.

Justin still didn't have a phone. He had programmed all his numbers in my phone. He grabbed the phone and dialed Gabe.

"Hey what's up?" Justin said as Gabe picked up. "Yeah we are doing this dinner tonight. Sorry for the short notice, but I totally forgot to invite you."

He paused as he listened, then continued. "Yeah. Try to wear something decent."

He paused again as he looked at me. "No, I don't think any random girls are going to be there. But you can still look nice for my wife and me, you punk."

I smiled with approval. The conversation continued.

"No I'm not saying dress up for another man. You know what? If you're going to be like that, I can un-invite you. No, it's cool. I was just trying to show my appreciation for you looking out for me and you totally turned it into something gay." He paused again as Gabe jockeyed him.

"Ok, see you at 8:30 punk. Don't call me babe. That's for my wife, you weirdo."

"So is Gabe confirmed?" I asked.

“I guess so,” Justin laughed. “But he isn’t sitting next to me.”

“No, that’s your friend. He isn’t sitting next to my people,” I said as I threw 10 different shirts on the bed. Justin was already dressed.

“Let’s figure out the seating arrangements right now,” I said. “Who is coming?”

“You, me, Tricia, Raymond…” he started.

“Rashon,” I corrected.

“You, me, Tricia, *Rashon,* Davis, Mandy, Gabe, and that’s it,” he said.

“Everyone can sit next to their significant other,” I said. “Tricia can sit between me and Rashon.”

“I’m not sure Gabe should be sitting next to some dude he never met before,” Justin said with concern.

“We can put Davis on the other side. It will be fine. Rashon is cool,” I assured.

“Oh really?” Justin asked.

“It’s not like that,” I said. “Tricia introduced us. We are all friends. He has some girl he’s talking to. He isn’t interested in me. You’ll like him though. He’s really chill. Kind of like you.”

“If you say so. Let’s go,” he commanded. It was only 7:45 according to the alarm clock on the dresser.

“We have time. Chill out. Let me get ready.” I pushed Justin out of the room. He grabbed the laptop to watch YouTube videos as he waited.

8:30 rolled around and we were late. Of course. Justin gave me a minute-by-minute update on the time as he pressed me to get out of the door. We finally got to dinner about fifteen minutes late and luckily, everyone was waiting outside in separate groups. Rashon and Tricia were chilling together on the bench in front of the restaurant as Davis, his wife, and Gabe loudly horse-played on the concrete sidewalk.

Tricia was elated to see me. Rashon was uneasy as usual, dressed up in a blazer, light colored V-neck and crisp, dark jeans. In contrast, Gabe wore a poorly ironed polo and jeans. He looked like the total brohe was. Davis, a short white Marine, wore a button down and sported his usual shaved head. His wife, Mandy, was a thick brunette with glasses. She was the typical military wife, having given birth to four babies over the past four years. She was a sweetheart.

Justin and I greeted our friends and merged the groups as we headed inside. Everyone exchanged uncomfortable hellos as we found our table. As everyone sat down in the order I planned, Justin and I grabbed Gabe by the shoulder and pulled him to the side.

I whispered to Gabe. “Please don’t embarrass us, Gabriel.”

He nodded.

“No jokes, someone here might actually be gay,” Justin added.

“What? No one’s gay,” I said in a loud whisper.

Gabe grinned, then responded. “On a one to ten, how far can I go?”

I gave him the *try me* face. “Three.”

Justin and I held hands as we set out to join the party. Gabe ran out in front of us. I knew I should have told him one instead of three.

"Ladies and gentlemen, may I have your attention please!" Gabe yelled. I put my head down.

"Oh no," I whispered to Justin.

"May I introduce to you Mr. and Miss Justin Rowland!" Gabe exclaimed as he applauded us walking arm in arm. Our table joined in the applause and soon, the entire restaurant was applauding us. My brown face was red with embarrassment. Gabe was too slick.

"Thank you! Thank you! Enjoy your meals!" I said to everyone as we seated. "Gabe I'm going to get you!" I said jokingly.

Everyone ordered drinks as we prepared for dinner. Gabe plopped down in his seat between Davis and Rashon.

"What's up?" Gabe said to Rashon. Rashon greeted him, then quietly browsed the menu.

"I'm guessing I'm the only person here that doesn't know anyone," Gabe said aloud.

I stepped in. "Davis, you know Gabe, right?" Davis responded.

"Sadly, I know him." Davis smiled as he grabbed Gabe by the shoulders. "You're not making a bad choice ignoring him," Davis said to Rashon.

"Oh, I'm not ignoring him. I just don't know what I want," Rashon said back.

"You're such a spiffy dresser," Mandy said to Rashon. He was uncomfortable with all the attention. A quiet thank you was all he could muster.

Everyone scoured through their menus and selected what they wanted. Tricia was uncharacteristically quiet. I leaned into her.

"What's wrong? You haven't spoken all night."

She smiled. "Nothing, girl. Believe me, nothing is wrong at all."

I studied her face. It said it all. She was getting some action from somewhere.

"No," I said. "Not what I think."

She blushed. "Momma gotta have a life too," she said jokingly. I giggled at the comment.

"That's disgusting," Rashon interjected. "I'm about to eat."

Tricia snapped back. "It wouldn't be disgusting if Kimberly was sitting here with you."

That hit a sore spot.

"We'll she isn't," he said solemnly.

Gabe broke the tension. "Who's Kimberly? If you don't mind me asking. Your wifey?"

Rashon shook his head. "Nah, just some girl. It's not important."

Gabe nodded. "I gotcha. The one that got away, right?"

Rashon looked on with an understanding gaze as Gabe kept talking.

"We all have that one that got away, bro. Don't beat yourself up about it. I'm single too, if any of the ladies were wondering. What's up, Tricia?"

"Now *that's* disgusting," I said. The whole table laughed.

"Nothing is wrong with flying solo," Justin said to comfort the conversation.

"True. But it's overrated," Rashon responded. "Do you know how much money I spend? You wouldn't understand. Single guys spend way more money doing things we wouldn't do if we weren't single like buying clothes, impressing women, dating…"

"I won't buy a chick a glass of water. She'll be a thirsty bitch messing with me," Gabe said. I gave him a look that said *check yourself.* Rashon laughed with him. They seemed to be hitting it off pretty well.

Tricia chimed in. She was not happy. "That's because neither one of you can handle a strong woman," she said.

"Here we go!" Rashon said as he threw his hands up. Davis and Mandy peered on as if they weren't even at the table.

"Here we go what?' Tricia said back.

"What makes you a real woman? Because you work to get free meals from a man you have no intention of ever being with?" Rashon asked.

Gabe jumped in. "Referee!" he said, looking at me.

I shrugged. I was used to Tricia going on her tirades.

"You just got to put yourself out there. You have to date a lot of pigs before you find your Queen," Justin said to Rashon.

"Don't try to earn brownie points," Gabe said. The whole table went quiet.

"Oh, my bad. I didn't mean *brownie points* like that. I'm brown too. Look at me! Venezuela all day!"

Everyone laughed at the comment. Our server came to take the orders. She was a cute Hispanic looking girl about our age.

Tricia nudged Rashon. "There you go!"

He shook his head. "I don't holler at females at their jobs. It's stupid. Nothing ever comes of that."

Justin chimed in. "You got to start taking shots. You never know until you know. I thought a black girl would never date me and look, *viola!*"

"How did you two meet?" Rashon said to include Davis and Mandy, who hadn't interjected anything in the crossfire yet.

"High school," Davis said proudly as he put his arm around his wife.

Rashon sighed. "Congrats. You're smarter than I. You got out the game early. There is nothing to pick from out here. You would be surprised how hard it is to meet people after you leave college and have to be a real adult."

"I can imagine," Davis said. "I've heard horror stories."

Mandy spoke up. "Everything in a relationship isn't always perfect. We've had our moments when we needed breaks."

"You guys look happy," Rashon complimented. "Enough about me and my problems. How is everyone else doing? What's new, Tricia?"

"Nothing much," Tricia said back. "I've been taking care of myself."

"Good. Good," I said. "That's what's important. Making sure you are straight before you bring anyone else in your life."

Davis interjected. "So how is everything with you two?"

A dark silence fell upon the table. Justin held his head down as I spoke up.

"Everything is great. Things couldn't be better," I said.

"They deserted me," Gabe said jokingly. Everyone laughed.

"You got the house all to yourself, bro. You can do whatever you want now," Justin responded.

"I was going to do that regardless. But man, sometimes I miss my dog. Many I miss my dogs!" Gabe joked.

"You know what? We need to do something special," he went on.

"Waiter, waiter!" he called out as he stood up to get her attention. Our waitress came back to the table, clearly slightly embarrassed.

"I want to order some shots. On me," Gabe said. "To Justin! To Kate!"

"You don't have to do this," I said.

"I insist!" he yelled.

The waitress brought back the shots on a round holder. Everyone took a glass.

Rashon spoke up. "I don't drink."

Gabe snatched his glass. "Music to my ears! Double shot for your dog!"

I put my hand on my head as I whispered to Justin. "It's going to be a long night."

Gabe led the toast as everyone downed shots. "To Justin and Kate!"

The evening went on as we enjoyed our meals, conversations, and the company of one another. For the first time in a long time, everything felt right. It was a wonderful dinner, minus how drunk Gabe got. He didn't stop at two shots. He didn't know how to stop.

Justin and I had to give him a ride home. I drove the Mustang with Gabe in the passenger seat as Justin followed us in Gabe's car.

"I'm sorry Kate," Gabe said in a drunken slur. "I think I drank way too much. But let me tell you this. You are a good woman. You are an f'ing good woman. Like, I know what happened. You have to be an f'ing trooper. You deserve an f'ing medal. So many women, especially in this town, would have been banging the next dude they saw. But you didn't do that. You're one of the good ones we were talking about. F'ing unicorn. You're like a beautiful black unicorn."

"Stop it, Gabriel. You're gone," I said. "There are things you say you'll never do or put up with until life makes you. You don't know what you're capable of getting through until you get to that point."

"You're a solider," he said as he gazed out of the passenger side window. The yellow haze of streetlights outlined his face.

"You're a solider!" he sang, imitating Beyoncé.

"You're too much. I appreciate you making the night special," I said. "Why aren't you married yet?" I asked him.

"Bitches, I mean women, are crazy," he replied in a slur. "Every chick I deal with is crazy, married, or both. I'm not trying to be that other guy bagging someone's wife then I'm the one hacked up in little pieces in the duffle bag because some crazy Marine can't take the fact his wife is a slore."

I didn't respond as he went on. "Every woman isn't like you Kate. A lot of these chicks got secrets and you won't even find out until you get on Facebook."

I replied quietly. "Yeah you're right. Bitches do be having secrets."

11

Then it happened.

It began like another regular day but at this point, I should have remembered my life was anything but regular. Justin and I's move back in together was successful until *the day.* Everything was going smooth. Justin was working, I was working. We would spend the evenings talking about life and politics while enjoying a home cooked meal. That was, until *the day.*

That day was extremely vivid. I got to work barely on time to which I found my co-workers in a panic. We had reports due and everyone was scrambling. I was a little ahead so I picked up the slack where I could. I was the office hero, which never happens. I remember my boss came over to my desk with a big, proud smile and told me, "Kate you've been a superstar. I know you can get the job done. I need to evaluate what everyone else is doing though. You are free to go. You have the rest of the day off, with pay."

This never happens. It was only 1:35, which normally was 10 minutes before I'd leave for lunch. I got off work early and the ominous day continued. Every light was green all the way home. This was unusual because the light to turn left out of our lot usually takes two or three minutes to change. That day it was smooth sailing, all green all the way home. It was almost like the universe was saying *you're going to deal with this today.*

When I got home, I saw the Furniture Depot truck. At first, I thought nothing of it. People move and buy furniture all the time. I've seen that truck all over the complex in the past but that day was different. The Furniture Depot truck was in front of *my* building. I pulled my car into a parking spot and locked on the truck as I got out.

"Hey, Foxy," the loud, rough voice yelled at me from behind. It was him. James. He was coming from the building with a tape measure in hand. His denim jacket didn't match his dark twill pants, nor the baseball hat he tried to hide his mane under. I tried to play it cool.

"What are you doing here?" I said with the largest forced smile I ever made in my life.

"Working. What's up? Long time, no hear." He put his hands on his hips as he stared me down. "Everything good with you?" he continued.

"I'm fine," I said as I decided whether to try to sprint to my apartment once his back was turned. "How are you?"

"I got fired from BP for leaving the store unattended that day," he said.

"Sorry to hear that."

He cut me off as he laughed. "Just kidding, I still work there. I just do deliveries on the side. My brother owns Furniture Depot."

I smiled nervously. "Congrats."

He chuckled. "Don't congratulate me, congratulate him. What are you congratulating me for? For having *two jobz!*"

James' references of black culture were hilarious but so refreshing.

"So what ever happened with your ex and the dog?" I asked as I folded my arms.

He shook his head. "Nothing. That's what happened. I would take her to court but it's a waste of time. Sometimes you got to move on to bigger and better things."

His eyes undressed my chest.

“Well, it was good to see you. You shouldn’t give up so easily on your dog. Get him back. I know he means a lot to you.” I said nervously as I tried to walk away.

“Hey Kate, what do you think? Can we hang out again sometime?”

I shrugged my shoulders. “I don’t kn-”

BOOM!

I heard my apartment door slam shut. The hair on my arms stood up. My stomach exploded. My knees turned into mush. Justin was here.

“Hey, babe!” Justin said as he embraced me.

James silently observed the interaction. I could tell he was determining what the relationship was between Justin and I in his mind.

“So the ruse is up!” Justin said as he looked at James.

James held a strong poker face. I damn near fell over.

“You can’t hide anything from a woman,” Justin said.

Justin decided he was going to surprise me. He had been saving up a little money by taking extra weekend shifts and decided he was going to take the initiative to order some new furniture for our place and of course *he had to order it from Furniture Depot.* My little bed was barely enough room for the two of us, but I wasn’t expecting him to actually drop cash on a new bedroom set. If only he and I knew the storm that would start.

James called my bluff. “So you know Kate, too?” he said to Justin.

I was had. The look on Justin’s face was one of intimidation and confusion. I was stone cold silent.

"Yes, I'm her… husband," he answered James.

"Oh really?" James said. "I didn't know you got married. *Congratulations.*"

That would normally be a harmless comment if Justin and I hadn't been married for years and coming off a separation. Point, set, and match. I was done.

"Well, you two look happy.Congrats again, Kate." James said as he hopped back in his truck.

Justin didn't say a word. His steel cold blue eyes pierced my soul.Once we got inside, the elephant in the room was too big to ignore. Justin was irate.

Justin screamed at me.

"Kate! Kate! Don't ignore me."

I hurried to the bedroom. The brand new bedroom set was a slap to the face of my integrity. I had no words, just tears, pain and guilt.

The tirade continued.

"You mean this whole time you were making me out to be the bad guy you were sleeping with some loser?!" Justin said.

"He isn't a loser," I replied.

"I don't care who he is!" Justin yelled. "Tell me, how long have you been seeing this guy?"

I tried to calm the situation. "Come on Justin, let's not go there. We are doing so well right now."

"Kate, answer the damn question!" he asserted.

"I have never slept with him!" I cried back.

"I don't believe you. That's why you were acting so funny that day we were there! Who else were you with while we were separated?" he asked.

"See Justin, that's why I didn't want you to find out," I said quietly.

He snapped.

"Find out what? I thought you didn't sleep together!"

I cried loudly. "We didn't! You need to calm down."

He breathed deeply. "Or what! You'll call the police on me again?"

BANG!

He pounded his fist on the round table.

"A man can only take so much, Kate. *I lost my whole life!* You were all that I had left. And you just took it for granted." He grabbed his temples and breathed in and out rapidly as he tried to control his rage.

I retorted. "As if you didn't have your fling?"

His head snapped in my direction like a coiled snake. "I owned up to it. I never ran from it. I told you exactly what happened. You already went through the text messages and all of Facebook. I have nothing to hide!"

He had had enough. Justin was losing himself. He quickly brushed past me and grabbed his car keys. I didn't even try to stop him.

BOOM!

He slammed the door on his way out. And like that, he was gone.

***

The next day, there was no sign of him before or after I left for work. All of his things were still in the apartment, completely untouched. If Justin moved out, he had left everything behind. Including me. I sat down in the middle of the kitchen floor, tired, angry, and lonely. The cold tile was chilling to the touch as I cried. It couldn't be over. I couldn't accept this.

KNOCK! KNOCK!

Someone was at the door. I slowly got up to see who it was. I prayed it was Justin, coming back to talk it out and move on. To my disappointment, it was just Tricia and Rashon. I let them in.

"Are you ok?" Tricia said as she locked on my fuzzy red eyes and tear-stained shirt. She gave me a big hug as she entered my apartment.

Rashon quietly added an "I'm sorry."

"We came over as soon as I heard," Tricia said. "Are you alright?"

I shook my head no.

She continued. "Has he been back?"

I responded. "No."

She looked overly concerned. "You have to get out of here in case he comes back. Pack some stuff up. You're coming with us."

I didn't even ask where we were going or what we were doing as I obeyed her command.

Rashon wandered around the apartment. He checked out my bedroom. "That's a nice bedroom set," he said.

"I wish I never thought about it. Stupid furniture ruined my life," I said as I ransacked my drawers for clothes.

“I never thought this would happen. I thought everything would be fine. Why me? Why does everything have to keep happening to me!” I cried.

Rashon sat on the edge of the bed.

“Sometimes it’s not about you. Sometimes things happen with no rhyme or reason at all and we just have to deal with it,” he added. It made sense but it angered me at the same time. I found my overnight bag and chucked it towards him.

“Help me pack,” I instructed.

Tricia joined us as Rashon packed some of my underwear in the bag.

“You guys are weird,” she said. ‘I’m saying ya’ll should rethink the dating thing.”

I gave her the look of doom.

“Too soon. Too soon. My bad,” she remarked. “But think about it.”

“Tricia I’m still freaking married!” I screamed. Rashon didn’t say a word as he packed the clothes I flung in his direction.

“Sorry girl,” she replied. “I haven’t thought of you as married since the incident first happened.”

She grabbed my laptop and sat down on the bed with her big butt covering all of the free space available.

“What are you doing?” I asked.

“While you two are picking out clothes, I am going to go on Facebook,” she responded. “Hurry up. He might come back.”

Rashon broke the hectic silence. “So Kate, how exactly did he find out?”

“James delivered the bedroom set,” I said softly.

“Damn,” he said. Tricia had her nose deep in Facebook.

“Justin updated his status. You might want to read this,” she exclaimed.

“Read it,” I said with a sniffle.

“No, you might want to read this,” Tricia said.

“I told you to read it,” I snapped back. “It doesn’t even matter at this point.”

“Ok,” she began.

“It is with great sadness that I must announce that my marriage is over. All of the work that I’ve done in the last six months has been for nothing. It is not my fault. I have done a deep amount of soul searching and I have come to the conclusion that people are not always who we think they are. I put my heart and soul into a relationship that was not what it appeared to be. Please with all due respect do not contact me further regarding this situation. What’s done is done and I cannot live a lie to please others. Thank you for your understanding.

God bless,

Justin.”

“He put all of that on Facebook!” I yelled hysterically. “Why does everyone have to know our business? This is insane!”

Tricia continued her fixation on the screen.

“Are there any comments?” I asked.

“Nah, no comments…” She continued to read.

"But what?" I said. "What aren't you telling me?" I sniffled. "Just tell me whatever it is."

"There is one like on the post," she said.

"Who!" I screamed. Tricia said nothing. She was sparing my feelings. I just wanted it to be over. I screamed again. "Who!"

"Sandra Young," she said. "Sorry, Kate."

My blood pressure boiled. My stomach exploded. I was beyond pissed. Rashon sat quietly, holding my now packed overnight bag.

"There is nothing that makes that ok," I said. "This is all f'd up. How could he post that for everyone to see?" I grabbed my temples. My head was throbbing with angst and anxiety. "His parents are going to see that. They probably all think I'm some no good black bitch now."

"I don't think that," Rashon interjected. I ignored him.

"You don't understand. He's trying to save face. That's what makes this so evil. It's not about him and what he did now, it's about what *that girl* did to him. That's all that post was about."

Tricia looked on. "I don't even know what to tell you girl," she said.

I stood tall as my headache subsided. I knew what I had to do. "Rashon, carry that bag for me please. Tricia, close that laptop. Let's go."

She was worried. "Go where?"

'We're going to find Justin. I want to talk to him face to face," I said.

***

About fifteen minutes later, we pulled into Gabe's neighborhood. I pointed out the directions as we swung around corners in Tricia's little blue Camry . We got to the house and parked along the street. There was no sign of the Mustang. I didn't buy it.

I got out of the passenger side. Tricia accompanied me as I walked to the front door. Rashon stayed put in the backseat of the vehicle.

KNOCK. KNOCK.

I banged on the door. No one answered.

KNOCK. KNOCK. KNOCK.

I pounded on the door harder. I could hear someone moving inside. I wasn't going to go away without speaking to someone.

KNOCK. KNOCK. KNOCK.

The door slowly creeped open.

It was Gabe. "What's up, Kate? How are you doing, Tricia?" he said with a forced smile.

"You saw Facebook. You know what's up," I said. "Where is he? Where is Justin?"

Gabe nervously answered. "He isn't here, Kate. I know you guys are going through some stuff but I'm not in it."

I didn't budge. I knew Justin too well. He prepared Gabe for my arrival in advance. "You're in it as long as you're lying for him. Now where is he?" I retorted.

He sighed. "Ok. You didn't hear this from me though. Justin is gone."

"Gone?" I said. "That's not good enough. Where is gone?"

He anxiously continued. "I'm not supposed to tell you this, but he left. He came by for like ten minutes and then left."

Something was still up. I wasn't getting the complete picture. Tricia butt in. "When did he come here and where did he say he was going? Stop playing with us, Gabe."

Gabe was taken aback by her energy. He didn't want any problems. He came clean. "About an hour ago, he came by to tell me you would be looking for him. He told me he was leaving town for good. He said he'd probably try to stay with his parents but he wasn't sure they'd let him."

I took a moment to take it in. Justin really had nowhere to go. "So he's going to Minnesota?" I asked.

"He seemed pretty serious about it," Gabe answered. "That's all I know, ladies."

A still tear rolled down my face. Tricia held a strong poker face. She was my backbone, and she was the only one not emotionally invested in hearing the facts. She was not fooled by Justin's setup as easily as I was.

She folded her arms and snapped at Gabe. "Where does this bitch Sandra live?"

Gabe was confused. "Sandra?"

Tricia got right in his face. She wasn't playing any games. Her neck popped and eyes rolled with each word. "Don't act like you don't know who we're talking about. Where does that bitch stay?"

Gabe backed down. "I don't know. I don't know her. I'm being honest. I don't hang out with that group. You'd have to ask Davis."

Tricia looked at me. She could see I was in deep thought. "Kate!" She snapped at me. "Do you know where Davis stays?"

I looked down as I thought deeply on where my life was headed. "Yes. I know," I said.

"Good. We are out." Tricia turned her back on Gabe without a word as we headed to the Camry.

"Hey Kate," Gabe called out from his door. I acknowledged him. "I'm sorry to hear about this," he said. I nodded as I got in the car to head to Davis and Mandy's home.

Fifteen minutes later, we were in the suburb on the opposite side of town, where Davis and Mandy's home was. They lived in a nicer neighborhood that was adjacent to a golf course. All of the homes were large residences with four car garages and neatly manicured lawns. It was the kind of place you dream of raising a family.

We pulled into Davis' empty driveway. He always kept his vehicles in the garage. I knocked on the door as Tricia and Rashon quietly sat in the car with the engine running.

KNOCK. KNOCK.

Mandy snatched the door open with glee. "Kate! Oh my God, I was not expecting you!" she said with a big, warm smile as she hugged me. Their children were scattered between daycare and school, so the place was unusually quiet. "Come on in!"

"I kind of can't," I said as I pointed to my friends in the car. "I just came by to ask Davis a question really quick."

Mandy looked confused. She must have not checked Facebook. She had no idea what was going on and I could tell my vibe was throwing her off.

“Ok?” she said. “Do you want me to call him?”

“I kind of need to ask in person. I need the real answer,” I said. She was still baffled.

“Ok. He is on his way home now. I can call him and tell him hurry up. He stopped to get some groceries on the way. I’m making stuffed peppers. You guys can totally stay for dinner if you want.” It was a genuine invitation, but we didn’t have time to accept.

“That’s fine. Maybe another time,” I said. “If you could call him, that would be good.”

Mandy plucked her iPhone from her pocket and dialed her husband. Her eyes had a look of overt concern behind her square-rimmed glasses. Davis picked up.

“Hello? Babe? Can you cut the shopping short? Yeah, I have Kate here. She really needs to talk to you. Ok, bye. Love you too!”

She looked back to the car. “Your friends can come in while we wait.”

We sat around their grand oak dinner table as Mandy insisted on serving us homemade iced tea. She was the ultimate host. You could just tell she was born to be a homemaker. She took great pride in every detail of her family and home from the perfectly framed crayon pictures on the refrigerator down to the spotless glasses our tea was served in. It was the type of life I once imagined for myself and Justin.

“This place is really, really nice,” Rashon said.

“You should come over more often,” Mandy replied. “We do a big Sunday football dinner. I make nachos and tacos. Consider yourself invited. Don’t be shy. Go Cowboys!”

THUMP. THUMP. THUMP.

The sound of boots clacking the hardwood floors quickly approached. Davis was here. He was still dressed in his cammies.

"Hey babe," he said as he kissed his wife and placed the shopping bag full of ingredients neatly on the counter. "What's up everyone?"

We all nodded and smiled as he joined us.

"I hear you need help with something?" Davis asked.

I softly spoke up. "I don't know if you know yet, but Justin and I had a big fight."

Davis leaned in to listen as I went on. "He left and I don't know where he is. I went by Gabe's and he isn't there. I think he's with Sandra. I need to know where she lives if you don't mind."

Davis leaned back and let out a loud sigh. He massaged his shaved head as he shook his head in disgust.

"I knew this would end bad," he said. "I don't know why they let Sandra in the group."

"I thought you're the one that knew her?" I asked.

"I was but it wasn't my idea for her to start hanging out with us. She invited herself. It was just no one said no."

Tricia and Rashon quietly looked on as Davis compartmentalized his train of thoughts.

"I can tell you where she lives but Kate, don't go over there and kill that girl. Don't do something stupid. I know you're upset."

"I'll try not to," I said.

"Alright. I'll write the address down for you," Davis replied. "If you need anything else, don't hesitate to come back," he added.

We immediately set towards Sandra's place. She lived about forty-five minutes away. The distance didn't matter. We were on a mission. Tricia put the address in her GPS as we hit the highway.

DING! DING!

"What's that sound?" Rashon asked from the backseat.

"We're good," Tricia said. "That's just my gas light. Don't worry about it. There's a BP station not too far from here."

12

Tricia rolled the blue Camry next to the BP station's gas pumps. Yes, *that* BP station, the exact same one I met James in weeks earlier. My back itched as the hair stood up along my spine. My elbows burned. Sweat rolled down my legs. I was having a full on panic attack.

"Do you want to get gas somewhere else?" I asked Tricia quickly.

"And run out of gas? I can't," she said. "Unless Rashon is going to push us to the next gas station. What are you worried about? I got this. You can pay me back whenever."

She had no idea it was deeper than BP's overpriced petrol. I slammed my head back on the passenger seat as I exhaled loudly.

"Kate? Kate? Are you ok?" Tricia asked.

"I'm not ok," I said.

"We are just going to go up there, see if he's there and go. You don't even have to knock on the door if you don't want to," she replied. My eyes cut to the double doors of the station as another customer walked inside. I peered deep into the store to see if I could see James.

"It's not that. Just hurry up and get the gas," I said sternly.

"You don't have to cop an attitude with me. I'm helping you out. I am not your enemy." I let her get the last word as she finally got out of the car to pump the gas. She shut the door. I turned to Rashon in the backseat.

"I have a problem," I said quickly.

"What's going on?" he asked in a confused haze. I probably knocked him from a daydream. He was quiet the entire ride. I looked back towards the store as I debriefed Rashon with instructions.

"Listen. I want you to go inside the store and buy something. Buy a few things. Get a lottery ticket or something. Just take a long time."

"Ok. I'll do it. But you're weird."

I shoved a handful of dollar bills at him. "Spend all this and be slow about it."

He took the money with the most perplexed look on his face. "On three, get out and I'm going to switch seats. One. Two. Three!"

We executed the plan to perfection. Rashon slipped out and I swam to the backseat. Tricia looked confused but kept pumping the gas. A minute later, she got back in the car as we waited on Rashon.

"What's the matter?" she asked.

"Headache," I said as I lay down across the backseats.

"I understand girl. I wish Rashon would hurry up!" Tricia said. Five minutes later, Rashon came back with a bag full of sodas and cigarettes.

"This is the best I could do," he said.

"Good," I responded.

Tricia fired up the car and we were back on the road. She headed for the direction the GPS lead us as we listened to the radio. About ten minutes later, Rashon broke the conversation.

"Oh yeah, Kate. I'm supposed to give you a message. Some guy said to tell you thank you. He got his dog back."

My heart fluttered. My eyes misted. I couldn't deal with the emotional typhoon in my chest. Feelings of being appreciated, abandoned, lusted after, and discarded all hit me at the same time.

I just smiled. "Oh yeah? That's cool. Thank you for telling me that."

"What's the deal with the dog?" Tricia asked.

"Nothing much. A friend of mine was going through some stuff with the courts and his dog. I'm just glad he got it all squared away."

The feeling was warm and heartfelt but it wouldn't last. We still had one more person to visit that day.

***

About thirty minutes later, we got to Sandra's place. It was an older apartment building in a small deteriorating college town. In a past life, I would have probably been too afraid to wander such a place but nothing was going to stop me today. Tricia found a spot alongside the street in front of the building. This place was a bit weird because the apartments were built on top of one another with outdoor entrances. It looked like a cheap two story hotel.

I got out and paced the area. My heart was beating out of my chest. Rashon and Tricia followed me as we rounded the street corners around the building.

"Kate, are you ok?" Tricia asked. I was beginning to get lightheaded. I could feel my eyes wanting to roll in the back of my skull but I was not about to give up now.

"I'm fine. I'm fine," I said. I scanned the area once again looking for the black Mustang.

"Hey, isn't that him right there?" Rashon said from behind me.

“Quit playing,” I yelled back as I turned my view. He wasn’t joking. There was Justin in his car, pulling up to the building. A woman was in the passenger seat. They got out and walked slowly to the building as they talked closely. The tear ducts in my face started to well up. It felt like I got drop kicked in the chest. Tricia grabbed me.

“I’ll call that bitch out right now if you want me to,” she said.

“That’s ok,” I answered, as they got closer and closer to the door. I spoke up as she reached for the door.

“Justin,” I said. He stopped dead in his tracks. Sandra snapped her head at us. I slowly walked over to their direction.

Sandra was a grungy, thin Mexican girl. Before today, I’d only seen her online. She was maybe 5’5” with short, messy black hair and tattoos on both of her arms. She looked like she stepped right out of a punk rock band. On this day, she stepped right into hurricane Kate.

“Justin!” I yelled. He just looked at me. He said nothing. “Justin! What are you doing? You’re just going to leave and run down here with this bitch!”

“Who are you calling a bitch?” Sandra said as she stepped to me. Justin held her back.

“It’s alright. This is my… this is Kate,” he said.

“Your wife!” I yelled. “Your wife,” I repeated more calmly. I couldn’t take it anymore. The dam broke. My face was drenched in my own tears.

“I don’t need to talk to you about anything. You wasted your time coming down here,” Justin said.

"I don't get it! We have one little fight and you disappear. We have one little argument and you leave me. I am your wife, who took you back after all that you did! Do you remember this?"

Justin breathed slowly from his nostrils. He struggled to maintain himself. "Kate. What's in the past is in the past. You know what you did and why I left."

I snapped at him. "As if you haven't been f'ing this bitch!" I screamed. Sandra stepped up again.

SMACK!

I let her have a right hand to the face. It was on.

Rights and lefts flew as I tried to instill as much damage as possible to make her feel my pain. I kicked at her, clawed her with my nails, and swung with everything I had as Justin tried to break it up.

"Get off of me! Don't touch me!" I hollered at him. My friends stood at the sidelines, waiting to jump in. Sandra continued to pull and scratch at me. She was tiny but came at me like she had four hands. The chick just wouldn't give up. Eventually, we were separated.

"So what? Are you with her now?" I said as I caught my breath. "Is this what you want, Justin?" He said nothing as Sandra looked on. "Huh? Say something!" I cried. He stood silent.

The tears burned in my eyes as I looked at him, standing there silent. It was his way of saying *I'm done*. It was in that moment I knew it was over. The loving bright blue eyes that once longed for me now held no emotion at all. He had completely checked out of the relationship. His trust was gone. A piece of his soul was dead. Something changed in him the day he met James, something that I couldn't repair.

I backed off the two as I turned to Tricia and Rashon. “Let’s go. I want to go.”

Tricia put her arms around me as we walked to the car. It was finally over. It felt like an atom bomb of disappointment went off.

“I’m sorry Kate,” Tricia said as we pulled off.

The following day, I drove in to my job from Tricia’s place and put in my resignation. It was time. It was time put the pieces back together. It was time to start a new life. I had to accept that Justin was over and life had to move on. I was free to stay with Tricia for a few weeks as I looked for a temp job to get back on my feet. I knew it was going to be hard but worth it in the long run.

***

“As soon as you sign these papers, everything is final,” Mrs. Powell said as we sat quietly at her desk. It was four weeks later and I hadn’t seen or heard anything from Justin until I got a random call from Mrs. Powell. Apparently, Justin hung on to the divorce papers I gave him and decided to sign, notarize, and deliver them to my lawyer’s office. He couldn’t even approach me for a divorce. The relationship was a cold war.

I took a deep breath as I signed my name next to his. Mrs. Powell stamped her seal on it, and it was done. I was officially divorced. It was the most anticlimactic event of my life. I thanked her for her time and got up to leave. She stopped me on the way out as she placed her round Coke bottle frames on her face.

“One last thing, I almost forgot,” she said as she pulled an unmarked envelope from her fuzzy fleece jacket. “I was told to give you this.”

It was a letter from Justin. I tucked the letter in my jacket as I headed out the door. The crisp spring air hit me in the face, as I felt somewhat renewed. Everything in my life wasn’t perfect but I had a lot to be grateful for. It was time to face whatever life had in store next. I pulled the letter out and read it under the afternoon's sun.

Dear Kate,

Here is what you wanted.

For the record, I never misled you and I never stopped loving you. It's just too great of a pain to be in a position where I cannot offer what you need. You deserve better. You know it, I know it, everyone knows it. I appreciate everything you've done for me. I am a broken man at best and I will never give myself permission to forgive myself for what I've put you through.

Friedrich Nietzsche once said "To live is to suffer, to survive is to find meaning in the suffering."

I hope that you can find peace and meaning from our time together.

With love,

-Justin

FIN

What's Next?

Let me know what you thought about the book!

Loved it? Hated it? Please leave a review at your favorite eBook retailer.
This helps me make each book better. Let your voice be heard!

Let's Connect!

Stay in the loop on future releases, updates, and special offers.

Join the exclusive email list today:

Click Here to Join

I will never spam you. I will only send love ☺

www.ingramcontent.com/pod-product-compliance
Lightning Source LLC
LaVergne TN
LVHW012111160826
845678LV00014B/3028

* 9 7 9 8 3 7 3 9 0 0 2 1 8 *